P9-DNM-437

MAR 2010

CH

The Girl Who Fell from the

Sky

a novel by

Heidi W. Durrow

ALGONQUIN BOOKS
OF CHAPEL HILL
2010

Published by
ALGONQUIN BOOKS OF CHAPEL HILL
Post Office Box 2225
Chapel Hill, North Carolina 27515-2225

a division of
WORKMAN PUBLISHING
225 Varick Street
New York, New York 10014

LIBRARY OF CONGRESS CATALOGING-IN-PUBLICATION DATA
  Durrow, Heidi W., [date]
    The girl who fell from the sky : a novel / by Heidi W. Durrow.
      p. cm.
    ISBN 978-1-56512-680-0
    1. Racially mixed children—Fiction. 2. Identity
(Psychology)—Fiction. 3. Intergenerational relations—
Fiction. I. Title.
    PS3604.U757G57 2010
    813'.6—dc22   2009027572

10 9 8 7 6 5 4 3 2 1
First Edition

*Dedicated to
my mother, Birgit,
with all my love*

If a man calls me a nigger
it's his fault the first time, but
mine if he has the
opportunity to do it again.
—NELLA LARSEN, *Passing*

PART I

Rachel

"You my lucky piece," Grandma says.

Grandma has walked me the half block from the hospital lobby to the bus stop. Her hand is wrapped around mine like a leash.

It is fall 1982 in Portland and it is raining. Puddle water has splashed up on my new shoes. My girl-in-a-new-dress feeling has faded. My new-girl feeling has disappeared.

My hand is in Grandma's until she reaches into a black patent leather clutch for change.

"Well, aren't those the prettiest blue eyes on the prettiest little girl," the bus driver says as we climb aboard. The new-girl feeling comes back and I smile.

"This my grandbaby. Come to live with me." Grandma can't lose Texas.

"Thank you, ma'am," I say. I mind my manners around strangers. Grandma is still a stranger to me.

I know only a few things about Grandma. She's a gardener. She has soft hands, and she smells like lavender.

For Christmas, Grandma always sent Robbie and me a card with a new ten-dollar bill wrapped in aluminum foil. On the back of the envelope where she pressed extra hard there'd be a small smudge. The card smelled like the lavender lotion she uses to keep her hands soft.

Grandma doesn't have a single wrinkle on her anywhere. She has eggplant brown skin as smooth as a plate all because of the lotion she sends for special from the South. "They got better roots down there—better dirt for making a root strong." Her body is a bullet. She is thick and short. Her dark hair is pulled back and is covered by a plastic bonnet.

"Well, aren't you lucky to have a special grandma," the bus driver says. "Pretty *and* lucky."

This is the picture I want to remember: Grandma looks something like pride. Like a whistle about to blow.

Grandma puts the change in for my fare. She wipes the rain off my face. "We almost home."

When we find our seats, she says something more, but I cannot hear it. She is leaning across me like a seat belt and speaks into my bad ear—it is the only lasting injury from the accident. Her hands are on me the whole ride, across my shoulder, on my hand, stroking my hair to smooth it flat again. Grandma seems to be holding me down, as if I might fly away or fall.

The bus ride is seven stops and three lights. Then we are home. Grandma's home, the new girl's home in a new dress.

Grandma was the first colored woman to buy a house in this part of Portland. That's what Grandma says. When she moved in, the German dairy store closed, and the Lutheran church became African Methodist. Amen. That part's Grandma too. All of Grandma's neighbors are black now. And most came from the South around the same time Grandma did.

This is the same house Pop and Aunt Loretta grew up in. On the dining room mantel are photographs of me and Pop. Of me and Grandma. Of me and Robbie. Of me, but none of Mor, that's mom in Danish.

"There, see that smile? That was the time I came to visit you over Christmas. Remember? Playing bingo. Oh! And I have a little present for you."

When she comes back, she holds a large wrapped box. I open the box. Make my first deals with myself. I will not be sad. I will be okay. Those promises become my layers. The middle that no one will touch.

"Thank you," I say and pull out two black Raggedy Ann and Raggedy Andy dolls.

"Aunt Loretta gave you her room. Dressed it all up in pink. Did you know that's her favorite color?"

I nod.

"And look at your hair. All this pretty long hair looking all wild from outside."

"We're gonna wash that tonight," she continues. "Your Aunt Loretta will help you. Bet she know how to do something better with that mess of hair than what you had done before. You're gonna go to school Monday and be the prettiest girl there."

She doesn't say better than your mama. She doesn't say anything about my mother, because we both know that the new girl has no mother. The new girl can't be new and still remember. I am not the new girl. But I will pretend.

THE TWO RAG dolls that Grandma gave me sleep at the bottom of the bed. Grandma and Aunt Loretta want to check on the poor baby. That's me.

I close my eyes and pretend sleep. I pretend sleep all the time now. "Poor baby, so tired." Grandma pats my hair.

It's the kind of hair that gets nappy. Grandma tried to brush it out before bedtime. I held real still, but it still hurt. She said I was tender-headed. The comb got stuck in the bottom in the back. Grandma said the tangled part is what's called my kitchen.

"She's got good hair. Leave her be." Aunt Loretta pulled the comb out, untangled each hair. "It's the same place where my kitchen is," Aunt Loretta said. "Where I get the naps in my hair too."

"Black girls with a lot of hair don't need to be so tender-headed," Grandma said. My middle layers collapsed. And I cried. And cried and cried.

Now my nappy kitchen head is on the pillow. All wild, like Grandma says. And I'm done crying. I don't want to be a mess or nappy or be so tender. "I'll wash it tomorrow, Mama," Aunt Loretta says. Her voice is honey.

I want to be as beautiful as Aunt Loretta. She smiles all the time even when she looks at the picture of Uncle Nathan. Her teeth are white like paper and straight. She shows her teeth when she smiles. I have a cover-up-my-teeth smile. Maybe I started doing it when Pop called me Snaggletooth.

Aunt Loretta is nut brown and knows she's beautiful. She was Rose Festival princess and got to meet President John F. Kennedy. Her skin is even prettier than Grandma's and she doesn't use that sent-for lotion.

Grandma and Aunt Loretta leave the door open enough to let light in. But still I press my back into the bed and open my eyes. No more pretend sleep. Now I will be real awake. Make sure the dreams don't come. Stay awake. Stay away from dreaming.

Tomorrow is my first day at a new school. I have a new notebook and pencils and a pencil holder with a zipper. I am going to think about school and practice the best cursive and learn all the big words I can know. I am going to concentrate. Be a good girl.

In my diary I write: "This is Day 2." Second day at Grandma's house. I wish I could go back home. Home to before the summer in Chicago. Back to base housing in Germany when there was me and Robbie and Mor and Pop. And everything was okay. Even though there wouldn't be an Ariel, that would be okay too.

Aunt Loretta makes pancakes special for me even though she has no business in the kitchen. Two pancakes and not enough syrup is what she gives me. Syrup that makes a stain in the pancake middle, gone so fast like the pancake is thirsty. I eat exactly what she gives me.

Aunt Loretta eats only one pancake. And Grandma none

because her teeth don't set right. There is something dangerous about pancakes because Grandma watches us eat. "How you gonna catch a lizard with your backside loading you down?" Grandma fusses at Aunt Loretta. I am smart and know that when she says "lizard" she means husband. That is called learning the meaning from the context. Because Grandma says it and she touches Aunt Loretta's face at the same time. That means she's talking about being pretty and being worth something and making it count.

Aunt Loretta laughs. And so do I. They are happy that I am laughing. It's the first time as the new girl.

"I don't need a lizard, Mama."

When Aunt Loretta says "Mama," I think of saying "Mor" and how I don't get to say it anymore. I am caught in before and after time. Last-time things and firsts. Last-time things make me sad like the last time I called for Mor and used Danish sounds. I feel my middle fill up with sounds that no one else understands. Then they reach my throat. What if these sounds get stuck in me?

I laugh harder, but the real laugh feels trapped inside too.

SCHOOL IS NOT a first-time thing. I sit in the front, where I always do. I sit quietly, like I am supposed to do. I raise my hand before speaking and write my name in the top right-hand corner of the paper. And the date. Because this is what good students do.

Mrs. Anderson is homeroom and language arts. She is a black woman. I think about this and don't know why. It is something I'm supposed to know but not think about. Mrs. Anderson is my first black woman teacher.

It makes me go back in my mind: Mrs. Marshall, first grade, favorite; Mrs. Price, second grade, not so nice; Mrs. Mamiya, third grade, beautiful; Mrs. Breedlove, fourth grade, smart; Mr. Engels, fifth grade, bald and deep voice. I remember they are all white.

There are fifteen black people in the class and seven white people. And there's me. There's another girl who sits in the back. Her name is Carmen LaGuardia, and she has hair like mine, my same color skin, and she counts as black. I don't understand how, but she seems to know.

I see people two different ways now: people who look like me and people who don't look like me.

"Rachel Morse?"

"Present."

"Where are you from?"

I answer: "4725 Northeast Cleveland Avenue, Portland, Oregon, 97217." I hear laughter behind me.

DAY 2 BECOMES Day 3. And the next day and the next. I count each day in my diary. Each day gets a new page.

Grandma thinks I am adjusting well. She says, "I think you adjustin just fine." I want her to put s's on the ends of her words and not say "fixin to" when she's about to do something. The kids in school say that, and I know they're not as smart as me.

There is a girl who wants to beat me up. She says, "You

think you so cute." Her name is Tamika Washington. She says, "I'm fixin to kick your ass." Sometimes she pulls my hair. In gym class she grabbed my two braids. I said "ouch" really loud even though I didn't mean to and Mrs. Karr heard. She said, "Tamika," and blew the whistle real loud. And Tamika said, "Miss K. I'm just playin with her. Dang." When Mrs. Karr turned away again that's when Tamika said it. "I'm fixin to kick your ass after school. You think you so cute with that hair."

I am light-skinned-ed. That's what the other kids say. And I talk white. I think new things when they say this. There are a lot of important things I didn't know about. I think Mor didn't know either. They tell me it is bad to have ashy knees. They say stay out of the rain so my hair doesn't go back. They say white people don't use washrags, and I realize now, at Grandma's, I do. They have a language I don't know but I understand. I learn that black people don't have blue eyes. I learn that I am black. I have blue eyes. I put all these new facts into the new girl.

And I am getting better at covering up the middle parts. When Anthony Miller kicks the back of my chair in class, I focus on the bump bump bump until he stops. I can focus on the bump bump bump and not say anything. I hear the smile on his face as he bumps my chair. Is he counting the number of times he can bump before I tell on him? I don't tell on him. And when Antoine mocks me in a baby voice when I answer the questions right, I don't have to cry anymore or be so tender. When something starts to feel like hurt, I put it in this imaginary bottle inside me. It's blue glass with a cork stopper.

My stomach tightens and my eyeballs get hot. I put all of that inside the bottle.

AUNT LORETTA BRUSHES my hair each morning and only sometimes makes pancakes. She's bought a special brush for me that's pink with white bristles. She holds my hair in her hands the same way as Mor did. Aunt Loretta's hands get lost in my hair. She has small wrists, tiny enough for me to wrap my fingers around. She has perfect red nails. She uses the nail on her right index finger to make the middle part. It doesn't scratch. She parts my hair from the front to the back to make the line. I feel the line she makes on my scalp. Grandma uses a sharp comb and it feels like she's dividing me in half.

TODAY IS SCHOOL picture day. Aunt Loretta wants to brush my hair special. I sit between her legs on her bedroom floor still in my favorite pajamas. Aunt Loretta smells of toothpaste and fresh white soap. I bunch my legs against my chest and wrap my arms around my knees. I feel like a boxer getting ready to fight in the ring. Not tender, just taken care of.

"Why do the other kids talk about my eyes?"

"Why?" Aunt Loretta says as if I should already know. "Because they're such a pretty blue."

I giggle when Aunt Loretta says this. A giggle can mean thank you or please stop looking at me. This time it means the first thing because it's school picture day and it's important to be pretty.

"Yeah, they're just like Mor's," I say, and I feel something like happy. I have said "Mor" out loud and made some of the inside sounds outside. I have said "Mor" and the glass inside me didn't shake.

I try the sounds again. "When Mor was little she had two braids in her hair too. *Hestehaler.* That means horsetails. I saw a picture." In the picture Mor is nine or ten or maybe eleven years old like me. She sits at a desk that opens up like a box.

"Well, today we're going to do something a little different," Aunt Loretta says. "Okay?"

I nod and know that it doesn't matter if I don't agree. I am a doll.

"I remember when I was a little girl," Aunt Loretta says. "I'd have to sit by the stove to get my hair pressed out. If I didn't smell the hair burning I knew it would be no good."

I have heard this story before. I think it's embarrassing but don't know why.

Aunt Loretta puts her nails in my hair and makes one part then another. She uses the big curling iron that goes in her hair even though my hair has curls. I smell hair burning.

I see a girl in the mirror when she is done, and she is not me. There are so many pieces to my hair. Nothing lays flat. There are stiff curls that don't wrap around my finger.

"You look like your grandmother spit you out herself."

I don't want to be spit.

I AM THE letter M and somewhere in the middle for class pictures. When I sit down, my feet don't reach the floor. My middle is all jumbled. I do my best cover-up-my-teeth smile, but the corners of my mouth barely move.

"Such a pretty black girl," the photographer says. "Why won't you smile?"

GRANDMA'S HOUSE IS two blocks away from the Wonder Bread factory, which means that my house is two blocks away from it too. What's hers is mine, she says. Simple math. Mr. Kimble, my math teacher, says that's what's called the transitive property.

Only I don't like what's Grandma's: an oily pomade she wears that smears my cheek when she kisses me, a green velvet couch with deep brown swirls that no one can sit on unless special company comes by, a porcelain music box decorated with people who look like kings and queens and a servant with a broken arm, a dresser full of fabric she's saving for the day I learn how to sew. Hers is the sent-for lotion, the rocking chair on the porch, and the pictures on the mantel, and the powder that looks like cornstarch that she puts in my underwear drawer. She has a lot more things but these are the main ones. Grandma is a collector. I think of her collections as junk and scraps. Like the other volunteer sorters at the Salvation Army, Grandma sets aside the good stuff for herself. Good stuff is a silver spoon, or a china teacup with or without a matching plate, or a dress-up purse with four beads missing and a torn strap. Grandma has boxes of mismatched coffee cups and saucers and yards of corduroy, gingham, silk, and lace stuffed into dozens of drawers and boxes in the basement. All these things are worth something but maybe only that Grandma sees.

Grandma's things are mine, and I am not allowed to touch

them. Only sometimes I do. Because how can you have something without holding it?

On Tuesdays we go to the Wonder Bread factory store and buy old bread even though it doesn't make any sense that the bread would be old because it comes from just next door. But maybe that's one of those things that works differently here in civilian life. That's what Pop would call it. He's a tech sergeant in the United States Air Force. He makes maps.

Civilian life is different than military life. In military life, you buy groceries at the commissary. Civilians buy groceries at "the store" even though that could mean Fred Meyer or the deli. Also in military life, you move a lot. Before we lived in Germany, we lived in Turkey. Pop never wanted to be stationed in the States. I don't know why. The good part about moving is you get to make new friends. The bad part is you don't see the old ones. Civilians live in the same house or apartment and know the same people their whole lives.

"Why would you want to live in the same place your whole life?" I ask my new friend Tracy. She's white. She looks at me like I'm crazy.

"You have to live where your parents live. That's just how it is," she says, and I make her not my friend anymore.

"I live with my grandma and my Aunt Loretta."

"So, that's different."

"I lived all over the world."

"No you haven't."

I open the blue bottle. Mad goes in there too.

YOU CAN BUY bread at the Wonder Bread factory store on a good deal. Grandma likes good deals. On Tuesday afternoon there's an extra discount and sometimes a few crumbled up cupcakes near the counter. They do not have *franskbrod,* or *rugbrod,* or *wienerbrod,* or any pastries with marzipan. They do not have the kind of bread Mor made. I wait for Grandma by the check-out counter. It's Tuesday but the crumbles at the counter are gone.

"This Roger's baby?"

"Mmm-hmmm," Grandma says to a tall woman wearing an African scarf on her head.

"No mistakin you in the same family. Roger got some strong genes makin these babies. Except for those eyes."

The new girl smiles a no-teeth smile when the African scarf woman takes her face in her hands. The new girl looks something like happy and stuck there. She's the trophy on Aunt Loretta's dresser with the perfect tennis swing. Smiling. Frozen. She is still. She is me.

Grandma grabs my face and wipes away imaginary crumbs from my mouth. I know they are imaginary. Grandma's just polishing me up.

"You know Roger's granddad had blue eyes. Something about like this." Grandma turns my head toward her when she says this. I am scared the sounds will spill out.

"They say that's the only way it can happen. What they call that?"

"Recessive," I say and don't know what other sounds might come out.

"She a smart girl. That's good. Just don't be too smart, young lady. The men don't go for that."

Grandma laughs.

The African scarf woman laughs and says, "We are a mixed up people alright."

"Mmm-hmmm."

"Makes you wonder what that boy would look like now," says the African scarf woman.

And Grandma says, "Either one of them boys. Or that baby girl."

Jamie

Jamie thought Robbie was a bird flying down below his window. He had been waiting for this bird and ran downstairs without calling to his mother, "Going outside," which is what his mother had told him to say even if she didn't hear him above the din of the television that played loudly in her room.

Jamie knew that his mother was not watching television. She had a new friend in there. Jamie knew the television as something that made sounds to keep the sound out. He was okay with that. The bird he had waited for had come. Of course, it didn't have to be this one, but it was. There were any number of birds that didn't belong in the Chicago sky.

There were two windows in his apartment. One faced the alley and the other the courtyard. Jamie didn't watch out the alley window. The things that he'd see fly by were never birds, but garbage bags hurled out the window from higher floors. They sometimes struck the air-conditioning units below. Whump. Sometimes catching there and rotting hot during the summer months.

Jamie, who was really James, was named after his father but not named Junior because he was really the third. Jamie wanted a strong name, like Steve or Brick. He had been Jamie since he was born, even though there was no way to confuse him with his father, James, a man he had met only in dreams. Jamie wanted a name with a different history.

Jamie who was really James ran downstairs to find the bird, to identify it, to see it. He would remember what he saw; he would write it down; he would record the date on his life list, the name of another bird.

IN HIS HANDS, Jamie held a book. It was the only gift he had ever asked for, but the book was not a gift. His birthday, July 23, came and went with no celebration and no cake and no gift.

Jamie got the book from the library. When the metal detector went off, he laid on the table a pocketknife he had found in the pants draped across the bathtub, the pants of his mother's new friend.

"Young man," the stout lady library security guard said, "you know you ain't supposed to be carrying this kinda thing around."

Jamie who was really James nodded. "I'm gonna keep this here until you come back round with your mama and she says it's okay for you to have it." His plan worked. He left behind the pocketknife, but took with him the *Peterson Field Guide to the Birds of Eastern and Central North America.*

JAMIE RAN DOWNSTAIRS with the *Peterson Field Guide.*

What is its shape? What shape are its wings? What shape is its bill? What shape is its tail? How does it behave? Does it climb trees? How does it fly?

Jamie had memorized these questions from the field guide. He repeated them so much in his head they seemed to have a melody. He knew the whole topography of a bird. His favorite part of the book was the beginning and the end, not as if the book held a story, but he loved the two sets of pictures of the birds' silhouettes. Number 13 was the magpie, 25 the meadowlark, 9 well, that was the mockingbird, and 14 was the nighthawk.

He was certain the silhouette of the great egret had passed his courtyard window.

He ran downstairs. One day he would leave this city and find more birds, Jamie thought, taking the stairs two by two and then sliding down the sticky banister on the last three-step flight before the door. He would fill up his life list with birds he could name and call.

When he finally reached the courtyard, he saw that his bird was not a bird at all. His bird was a boy and a girl and a mother and a child.

The mother, the girl, the child. They looked liked they were sleeping, eyes closed, listless. The baby was still in her mother's arms, a gray sticky porridge pouring from the underside of her head. The girl was heaped on top of the boy's body, a bloody helpless pillow. And yet there was an old mattress, doughy from rain, just ten feet from the bird-boy's right arm, which was folded like a wing beneath him.

Pain moved the boy's body. His bones jutted from his wrists. His eyes were wide open. He can see me, Jamie thought.

The boy seemed to have landed feet first on the sodden cement courtyard filled with garbage bags bursting with scent and refuse. The bones from the bottom of the boy's leg poked through his jeans at his thigh. He lay on the ground on his back as if he had fallen from a large, comfortable nest.

It was not until the policemen came and raked through the courtyard's waste that Jamie could turn away. The policemen collected matchbooks, soda bottles, and empty brown paper bags, scraps of paper, and other possible clues: a jack of clubs playing card lying on a brown-stained sheet, and a ticket from Saturday's Quick Pick Lotto. Jamie was still holding his *Peterson Field Guide*. He had no names for what he saw.

Laronne

These white girls, Laronne thought despite herself. These white girls think all they need is love.

When Laronne heard what happened, she made herself family. Laronne convinced the building super to let her up. "She's my sister-in-law," she said. "They were my babies too." But she hadn't had to lie. Laronne's was the only contact name on Nella's rental application, under "employer."

"Maybe you can find something they couldn't," the super said.

In the four weeks since Laronne had hired her, Nella had always been on time. When she didn't show up that Tuesday morning, Laronne called to find out what was wrong. Nella did not answer the phone.

Nella had seemed distracted the last few days. The baby—just six months old—wasn't sleeping. And the boy, he wasn't feeling too well. And Nella's daughter—such a little lady—she was beside herself because there was no money to visit the amusement park before the summer's end as Nella had promised. Laronne couldn't make everything better, but she had fifty dollars to lend for the kids to enjoy the park's big rides.

"I know you worry about them—new to the city and all—but kids can't be cooped up watching TV all summer," Laronne had said. "Go on, take this. And don't worry none about when you get this back neither. Go and you and the kids have some fun."

Laronne was happy to help. Over the years, she'd become quite the hen-mother to her employees in the community college library. When they had no place to go on holidays, she insisted they crowd her dinner table. A couple of times an employee had come to live with her just to get through a tight month. And her son had grown used to seeing piles of presents under the Christmas tree—all meant for his mother's employees and their families.

Laronne's husband sometimes chided her for getting too involved. "You're the boss, not the mom." But Laronne knew that her employees—mostly young mothers newly divorced working outside the home for the first time—were all working on a second chance. If she could do any small thing to help, she would.

Nella took the money and smiled. It was the same wide smile Laronne remembered when she told Nella she had the job.

"I am new in the city," Nella said "I was thinking . . . I

thought—Roger always said it would be hard. America was not what I thought it was. Thank you. Thank you."

Laronne laughed.

"Oh, child. It isn't easy. Especially not this town. Can't imagine picking it over where you're from."

In her first days at the job, Laronne learned that Nella had left Germany and her husband for a man, an American contractor she'd met at an AA meeting near base.

She fell in love the night he drove her home in his beat-up Benz after a group potluck, but got lost with the directions she gave. It was the kind of thing that could have set Roger into a rage. Why couldn't she just learn to read a map? But Doug said they'd have to figure out a different way to get her home. He stopped the car, walked over to open her door, and said: "We'll just navigate by the stars."

Oh, these white girls, Laronne thought.

Two weeks ago Laronne had found Nella in the bathroom curled into a ball, crying. She shook with every breath like a fist was opening up inside her.

"Laronne," Nella had said, "I thought it was right. I do not know what to think. Feel." Laronne had never been one to counsel or advise, but she saw that Nella needed some words, any words: "Just pay attention to what happens in here," she had said, making a circle in the center of her chest with her hand. You can't tell a grown woman what to do no way, she thought. "And take care of yourself and those kids," she said. "That's all you got to do."

It was slightly before noon when the white man, with his bright orange hair slicked back, came into the library with a bouquet of flowers in his hand, asking for Nella. This was the man Nella had left her marriage for?

"I'm afraid I can't help you," Laronne had said.

"Ma'am," he said in a lowered tone. "I need to see her. To give her these."

Laronne wasn't one to be bullied.

"Sir," she said with equal force. "I'm afraid I can't help you. But maybe security can." He stood there glowering at her for a moment before he stormed away.

Laronne could feel her heart quicken but more from anger than from fear. Nella's got to handle her business, Laronne thought. But not here, and not on my time.

WHEN LARONNE LEFT a second message for Nella that afternoon, she hesitated for a moment, and then, instead of saying "How are you?" or "Can I help?" she said, "Don't bother coming in tomorrow. We won't be needing your services here anymore."

What more did Laronne owe her? What more did she have to do?

IT WAS A gray August evening. It had been a wet August day. As Laronne stepped into the apartment's light, shadows of the couch rose up on the walls. The large green couch, a bassinet, and a television were the only pieces of furniture in the room. There were no bookshelves or tables or decorations—just opened suitcases along the wall serving as makeshift dresser drawers and dozens of moving boxes, some unsealed, most of them full.

In the bedroom Laronne could see which child had slept on

which side. The girl had made a nightstand out of an empty box. Her pajamas were folded and tucked beneath her pillow. Her bed was made. Library books were stacked neatly by the mattress on the floor.

Laronne turned over the box that served as a nightstand and put the girl's belongings inside. Three stuffed animals, a few sweaters, two pairs of pants, and a pair of dress shoes.

Everything would have to be packed away.

FROM THE KITCHEN window Laronne saw the crowd that had gathered before the courtyard cordoned off by the yellow police tape. The crowd stared up in the air as if looking for signs. They drew lines in the air—flight patterns of a family that fell from the sky.

It was the Tuesday after Nella's first payday and the cabinets were nearly bare. Laronne trashed a can of coffee, two white boxes of macaroni and cheese, a sweet cereal, and a dented tuna can. In the refrigerator was half a pitcher of orange juice, a baby bottle, applesauce, ketchup, and a box of the orange government cheese. Laronne threw it all away.

It was in the drawer by the stove she found a pad of paper, pens, uncut sheets of wallet-sized school photos of the boy and girl, scissors, and five ten-dollar bills paper-clipped together along with a note.

Dear Mrs. Warner,

Thank you for giving us the money to go to the amusement park. We are going next week. I can't wait.

Love,

Rachel

Nella had paid her back.

Laronne retrieved the coffee can from the trash. She emptied out the grounds. With the scissors she cut a hole in the coffee can lid. Then she marked the can with tape COLLECTIONS and stuck the ten-dollar bills inside. This would be for the lone survivor, the girl.

Rachel

Aunt Loretta plays tennis on Sunday mornings with a possible lizard named Drew. "At least he ain't funny, like that Nathan turned out," Grandma says. "But he still keepin you away from the Word." That's Grandma's way of yelling. She doesn't make her voice go loud or hard, just makes the sounds go capital. "BUT, he STILL keepin YOU AWAY from the WORD." Aunt Loretta never goes to church. Not since Uncle Nathan went away.

Grandma goes to the AME church every Sunday morning and sometimes Wednesday nights too to "lift up" one of the church ladies if someone's sick. Today she's giving Aunt Loretta the devil because she's not going with us to raise up the Lord's name.

"You're the one that wants me married, Mama. You're the one that made me play." Aunt Loretta isn't defensive when she says this. She talks with facts. She has a high school tennis trophy on her dresser from 1967 and a date with Drew to play.

Playing tennis is one of the things that goes in the white category, along with classical music and golf. Tamika said that in PE when Mrs. Karr was teaching us how to understand the score.

Tamika is no authority, but I noticed the other black girls agree. The only black people I've seen play tennis are Aunt Loretta and Pop. And they're related to white people, to me. I don't ever mention that I'm related to white people. And most of the time I try not to let the black girls like Tamika see me talk to Tracy, because Tracy is a white girl. And the way they say that—*white girl*—it feels like a dangerous thing to be.

But Grandma always wanted Pop and Aunt Loretta to know white things. Like when Pop wanted to be a musician. Grandma made him play the piano, when what he wanted to play was the banjo or harmonica. A piano is more white than a harmonica. I don't know if it was a secret from Grandma, but sometimes Pop still played the harmonica too.

Grandma can't argue with Aunt Loretta. She does want Aunt Loretta married. She does want her to have something more. But sometimes it seems that Aunt Loretta has a different more in mind than Grandma. Grandma's more for Aunt Loretta is a good secretarial job, a husband, two children and a house nearby.

That kind of more doesn't seem enough for Aunt Loretta and probably not for me.

Aunt Loretta's boyfriend, Drew, is her new tennis partner. Drew is handsome and not a boyfriend that gives anyone looks. Drew likes Aunt Loretta because she's 1) pretty of course, 2) a good tennis player, and 3) smart. I've never heard boys say this was a good thing before.

I like Drew because he is smart and he has a big, deep voice. He talks about "giving back to the community," "uplifting the people." He says the things he says over and over. He is very passionate the way he talks—more even than a preacher or a person running for president. Drew works downtown at the Salvation Army Harbor Lights Center. He is a drug and alcohol counselor. He says the same things Mor said. "Easy does it." "One day at a time." That kind of thing. It's a code language. And I know what it means.

I also like Drew because he makes the happy in Aunt Loretta more visible. The bus driver, the mailman, even the grocery store cashier at Fred Meyer can see it. It's not different for Aunt Loretta to smile—she does that all the time. It's easy to smile just to make other people feel better. But when a person fakes happy, it has edges. Regular people may not see, but the people who count, they can see edges and lines where your smile ends and the real you, the sadness (me) or the anger (Grandma), begins. The lines and edges are gone from Aunt Loretta when Drew is around. And the picture of Uncle Nathan on the mantel is gone too—the one where he's leaning into Aunt Loretta and it looks as if he can't get the question off his face. That's a good thing, I think. You shouldn't hold onto things that give you edges. Now there's more light inside Aunt Loretta, inside light that other people can see too.

AT SCHOOL I HAVE the best cursive handwriting, and I am learning more big words like *discombobulated* because Mrs. Anderson always says that.

"You've got me all discombobulated," she says when she smacks the yardstick on Anthony Miller's desk and breaks it in half. That makes Anthony Miller laugh even harder.

Today when Anthony Miller does the bump bump bump against my chair, I turn around and make my face very still. "I'm not going to tell on you," I say to Anthony Miller, which makes him smile with dimples so deep they can hold new nickels.

"Sorry," he says "for bumping your chair." The space between his eyes seems smaller than before. His forehead squishes together. "Does it hurt?" he asks and his smile changes. I could look at the poster above his head on the back wall or at the blue-ink squiggles he's made on his paper instead of the answers to the vocabulary test on the board, but I look him in the eye even though the blue bottle is open and the heat fills my face. "Not," and my tongue is Robbie's, "r-r-really." I can't stop the cry that wants to come. I haven't. Anthony Miller's eyes open wide like I've given him a special Christmas present.

I don't like it when I surprise myself by crying. The only time I do it really is when I wake up from a nightmare like last night when Robbie was with me in my dream. He was Robbie but he wasn't Robbie. He had black hair like matted yarn and big brown eyes (not green) that looked like buttons stitched on wrong. He smiled at me a little crooked, and I tugged at the edge of his mouth to get him to laugh. But his smile turned into a thread in my hand. I picked at every loose thread, and then his face was empty. Only needle holes were where his eyes, his nose, his smile had been. There was no way he could cry or even scream. So I did. *Robbie!*

Aunt Loretta always comes to check on me if she hears me scream in the middle of the night. "Poor thing," she says. "It's alright. Go ahead. Let it out."

Sometimes Aunt Loretta seems more scared of my nightmares than me. Aunt Loretta says, "What happened to you, it was scary. It was a scary thing that . . ." She doesn't know what to say.

"It's hard to make sense of," she says. "But you're safe here."

"Okay," I say without disagreeing. I am what she calls "safe," and to me I am what I call "waiting." In my diary I keep counting the days. I am waiting for Pop to come back—for Pop to come get me and take me home. Not to Germany. Not to where we spent that summer in Chicago. Not Denmark where Mor said she'd never go again. Home—wherever Pop is—even if it's just me and him.

The words on the board look fuzzy right now. If I concentrate I can copy down number 2 *invade* and then number 3 *invalid*. I am at *inundate* and Anthony Miller says, "Here," and bumps my right arm making my *u* go jagged. He gives me a cafeteria napkin, crumpled from his pocket. It's in my hand already when Mrs. Anderson comes toward Anthony Miller.

Crack. Mrs. Anderson's yardstick smacks down on his desk and breaks in half. The crack is in my bad ear. I can feel it pulse red because there is nowhere for the sound to go.

"Hush. It's time to be quiet." Everyone is laughing and not

at all quiet. This is the third yardstick Mrs. Anderson has broken this week, two of them on Anthony Miller's desk.

"It was me again Mrs. A. Sorry," Anthony Miller says. "Sorry" sounds different now, or I make it sound different. I hold onto Anthony Miller's first "sorry," the one meant for me. *Does it hurt?* No one asked that before.

I am still counting days.

WHEN GRANDMA IS gardening is the only time she doesn't seem just a little bit mad. Even when she wakes up in the morning, there's a frown on her face. Grandma wakes up at 5:15 a.m. She takes the number 7 bus downtown and transfers to the 34. That takes almost two hours. She works for a white lady in the southwest part of town. That's where the white people live. None of them have time to take care of their grandmothers, and that's what Grandma does. Grandma is a grandma who helps grandmas. That seems important. When Grandma needs help, I don't want another grandma to take care of her. I'll do it myself. I think that's only fair.

When Grandma is gardening, I sit on the porch in her rocking chair and read. Right now I am reading Chaim Potok's *The Chosen.* One girl in class said it was the first big book she has ever read. I've been reading big books since fourth grade. I have some favorites. I think this book will become one of them.

"You think I don't like books," Grandma says. I never said that. But I do wonder sometimes when she asks me to read her the listings in the *TV Guide:* Maybe Grandma can't read.

"Grandma, you just know things." I say this like I am giving her the pat on the head that she wants. Grandma does just know things—like she knows the names of the flowers and plants. She can see only the leaf and tell you what it's from and what it can do.

Aunt Loretta is different than Grandma. She's interested in things, new things—not just gardening, good deals, looking respectable, and being clean in pressed clothes. Aunt Loretta doesn't talk the way Grandma does either. She makes her *t* and *ing* sounds sharp. There is no Texas in the way Aunt Loretta talks.

Aunt Loretta has something that maybe you could call class. It's not the made-up kind like Grandma has, fake pearls and Sunday hats, but something that comes to you as if you were born to the king and queen. Aunt Loretta understands better than Grandma that reading a big book is more classy than wearing fake pearls watching TV. I wish I knew a better word for what I mean. On the days she's feeling fussy, Grandma calls it "High Falutin" and then she calls it "white"—like the kids at school.

When Grandma fusses at me, it means she wants me to like her. I will like her enough. Sometimes I can even say, "I love you, Grandma," and that means something to her. I do love her because I have to. She's my grandmother.

I have a trick figured out though, so I don't make mean thoughts about her when she starts to fuss. Thoughts like she's not so smart, like she's not as good a mother as Mor. I picture Grandma my age and someone loving her. I picture someone loving her but not someone like me who can curl into her lap while we're watching TV, and I'm loving her soft squishiness, and her lavender, and the little bit of sweat I can smell if she's still wearing her blue dress uniform. I picture someone loving Grandma small. Grandma curled up. Grandma closing her eyes when a warm hand runs through the front of her hair. Grandma's hands are the ones that are quiet, and the loving one's touching her.

"It's true. I don't know any of them books you be readin," Grandma says. "But I would of if they let me go to school. To that private school."

There is a story there that Grandma doesn't tell. It's a story that makes her sigh and tut-tut. When she digs again, she is in that story, not looking at the ground, but pictures of Texas in her mind. Or maybe they are pictures of herself young, more like Aunt Loretta—more like a girl who was going somewhere. That's when she stops looking so mad.

"Grandma, I think if I read you the stories, you could have the same books in you too."

"You think too much," she says.

"Don't listen to that. You keep on making your mind good. That's important," Aunt Loretta says.

She's come home from work, an office job where she types and gets coffee or lunch for the boss. She's still in office clothes: a skirt, high heels, a silk blouse, and a sweater. Seeing her standing on the porch right then, it's hard to imagine that Aunt Loretta even belongs here.

You can see how she looked exactly right driving down the street in Los Angeles in a fancy car or riding in a cab in New York City, when she was married to Uncle Nathan.

"My mother means well, Rachel, but you just keep doing

what you're doing with your studies," Aunt Loretta says. "It's important."

"Ain't nobody said it wasn't. But she need to put some common sense up against that book sense."

"Mama, leave her alone. She's a good girl."

"I'm right if I say they used to say that about you too," Grandma says. "Still you run off just seventeen with that boy Nathan. You slept in the bed you made."

Grandma and really no one talks about where Uncle Nathan went. Uncle Nathan played football and basketball and baseball. "Real good," as Grandma says, meaning very well. Uncle Nathan doesn't play anything now. His "playin around days" are done. I don't think he died because then Grandma would never say his name. "Bad luck conjurin up spirits and all." Grandma never says "Ariel." Grandma never says "Robbie." Grandma never says my mother's name.

I have never seen Aunt Loretta look anything like mad. Sad is what she does normally, but right now in her eyes it's as if all she is is a flame. But she doesn't say anything. And then it's like someone's thrown water on her. "You know what, Mama," she says, "you're right. You go on and be right."

Jamie

Jamie visited the courtyard shrine every day until it rained.

The shrine was made of an old board elevated by two cement blocks a foot off the ground. On the board, covered by a brightly colored cloth, there were candles, flowers, a teddy bear, and balloons—two already popped—attached with barely sticky tape. And there was a coffee can with a hole poked through the plastic lid, like the one passed around at church, that said COLLECTIONS.

On that first day, Jamie put a quarter in the coffee can. He wanted to put in more.

A school portrait of the bird-boy was taped to the collection can. In the photo he was six maybe seven, Jamie thought, because he was missing the same two teeth Jamie was missing at that age. And next to that was a photo of the girl with the fuzzy hair and the blue blue eyes.

There was also a framed family photograph. The mother was seated in a wicker chair and standing on each side were the boy and the girl. It was the family from the sixth floor. Jamie had seen them when they moved in a few weeks ago and in the stairwell a few times too. It was summer, but he never saw them play outside.

What is its shape? What shape are its wings?

THE TELEVISION CAMERAS came on the first day. Channel 2, 5, and 7 interviewed neighbors Jamie had never seen. The neighbors said many things:

She seemed regular.
Kept to herself.
Always made sure those kids were clean.
Cute kids, damn shame.
Polite, quiet.
Didn't know much about her.
She had a man around here for a while. A white man. Kinda scraggily lookin.

Acquire the habit of comparing a new bird with some familiar "yardstick"—a House Sparrow, a Robin, a Pigeon, etc., so that you can say to yourself, "smaller than a Robin; a little larger than a House Sparrow."
What is its shape?

THE NEXT DAY the shrine was still there. The cameras were gone.

The coffee can that said COLLECTIONS remained—no thief brave enough to steal money meant for a grave.

The yellow police tape that cordoned off the spot where the bird-boy and his family had lain was torn. Part of it had blown away, and the rest flapped in the wind.

Jamie had emptied his mother's pocketbook. He had run his hand beneath the couch cushions. He walked along the sidewalk looking for loose coins. Including the six beer bottles he turned in for change, he collected $5.83. He put the money, two fistfuls of coins, in the collection can.

Jamie who was really James stood before the shrine thinking of his life list. It was still a list of ordinary birds: robins, sparrows, pigeons, gulls. The great egret, snowy white, airborne. If only that was what he had seen that day. He would have become someone worth knowing. He would have been in the newspapers, maybe even on TV. How could he have been so wrong? How could he have made the shadow of a boy into a bird? There were questions he had to learn to ask, to train his eyes to see.

What shape are its wings?

He stood before the shrine for hours that day. When he finally went home for dinner, he was surprised to see his mother seated on the couch. She called him to her and hugged him close. She cooed: "You okay, baby?" She rocked him back and forth. She was yeasty and pale. No new friends in the last three days and his mother needed touching.

Her arm dangled limply across his shoulder. "Your mama's not so bad, is she?"

He took the love she gave, the broken pieces of affection. Maybe the bird-boy had changed things after all. "Mom," he said, "I saw—"

Just then the bedroom door opened. A new friend stood in the doorframe. "What you waitin on, girl?"

Only then did Jamie see the familiar marks on his mother's arm and the haze that she seemed to be seeing him through, the glassy look in her eyes. The feeling that rose between them became a chasm, an opening wound. How could he ever be certain of what he saw?

There were questions he had to learn to ask, to train his heart not to feel.

His mother retreated to the bedroom. "Mama's gonna go rest. Tell me if you go outside." The sound that kept out the sound played.

"Going outside," Jamie said a few moments later. He grabbed his book and walked down to the second-floor landing where he sat and read.

Learn bird songs. They can identify a species even when the bird may secrete itself in thick cover.

Jamie thought: He could have known the new new friend was there. He thought: Had he listened for the sounds, he would have heard thick shoes on the bare parquet floor, the belt clasp undone, and its click on the opening zipper. He would have heard the folding down of sheets. He would have known his mother's limp hug was pure apology.

AFTER TWENTY MINUTES in the stale stairway — minutes that felt like hours as he waited for the new new friend to leave — Jamie walked downstairs, then slid down the banister to the landing. A man with woolly-looking orange hair sat rocking back and forth, blocking the path to the door.

"Excuse me." Jamie's voice was so small the man batted it away as if it were a fly. "Excuse me," he said, a little louder.

"What?" The orange-haired man looked up. His eyes didn't focus right.

"I just need to . . ." Jamie's voice trailed off as the man scooted to the side.

Jamie ran to the shrine where half a dozen people were gathered.

A reporter—pretty and young like his first schoolteacher— wanted to make the bird-boy's story one that made sense. The reporter tried to coax out their stories the way Mrs. Gordon had when she wanted the kids to say their ABCs. Still no one would talk to her. Then she approached Jamie.

"Hey," she said. "Did you guys play together? You and the boy?" she asked.

"No," he said. He hugged the *Peterson Field Guide* tightly against his chest as his armor.

"Go to school together?"

"Huh-uh."

The reporter wrote "no."

There were questions she should ask, Jamie thought. These were not the ones.

"What did you see?"

I saw a bird, he wanted to say. A great egret in the sky. I saw it swoop down below my window. I wanted to see it land.

Jamie who was really James didn't give that answer. What did he see? It didn't matter. His eyes saw everything wrong. Shadows, mothers, birds.

Instead he said, "I saw a man. At the top of that building. He pushed them off and ran."

The reporter asked him more questions and he answered.

Jamie who was really James was shaking inside with delight. The reporter wrote down every word he said.

"Yes, ma'am," he said. "That's exactly what I saw—the way it happened."

"Great." She continued scribbling. "Did you tell the police?"

"Ma'am?"

But the reporter had forgotten the question as soon as she'd asked. She turned and said to the photographer, "I want a picture of him."

"Could you hold this up?" the photographer asked Jamie and handed him the framed family photograph from the shrine. Jamie's hands were trembling with excitement.

"What's your name, sweetie? And tell me how to spell it," the reporter asked.

Jamie thought of the great egret, of his life list, of his father James. He thought of how much he wanted a new history to his name, and he said, "My name's Brick. I'm eleven. B-r-i-c-k."

THE NIGHT JAMIE who was really James became Brick he could hear the rain on the courtyard window. He heard the wind and the clank of metal garbage cans that had lost their lids. *Learn bird songs. The call note, the song.* Jamie hummed himself to sleep, a tune buzzing into his dreams.

In the morning he left without eating the cereal his mother had left for him. The milk was warm and the bowl was half full of cornflakes that were mostly crumbles. He ran to the newsstand by the bus stop to see the morning's paper. Page B3. His was the hand that held the photo of the bird-boy's family. When the newsstand man turned, Jamie ran off with just the B-section in his hand.

"Hey!"

Brick ran faster. Finally, two blocks away, he stopped and read the story. He sounded out the big words. He read his new name.

THAT AFTERNOON JAMIE saw that the shrine had not survived the night's storm. The rain had soaked what was left: the teddy bear, the candles, the family portrait in the frame. The coffee can was gone. Jamie who was really James picked up the board and perched it on the cement blocks again. The soggy teddy bear squished like a sponge. He poured the water from the candles' burning wells and wiped the water from the family portrait, now wet beneath the frame's glass.

Jamie who was really James but who was now Brick placed the *Peterson Field Guide* on the shrine next to the bird-boy's family photograph. He didn't want the field guide any longer. From now on he would simply listen. He would know things even when his eyes were closed. He would know them by sound.

Laronne

After work the next day Laronne visited the courtyard.

Without the flash of the police car lights, or the television crews, the crowd had thinned. An elderly black man set a bouquet of carnations on the shrine and stuffed a bill in the collection can Laronne had made. He paused, also, to pick up the framed photograph Laronne had taken from Nella's desk at the library and placed in the shrine's center.

Laronne recognized the man from one of the television reports. He was a neighbor of Nella's who had helped bring up the groceries one afternoon. "Her place was spic-and-span clean," he had said.

All day Laronne had heard the same kind of whispers at the library where she worked.

She was real helpful.

I thought she was really smart.

Sometimes I couldn't understand her accent.

She always seemed so nice.

The collection of whispered comments and impressions didn't add up to a story that made sense of what happened; they could hardly be considered clues. What people wanted to know was why Nella had turned so dangerous. Why hadn't the danger been seen?

Laronne saw a light-skinned, curly-haired boy as he approached the shrine. He lifted the collection can gingerly and into it dumped two handfuls of coins. Had he lost his best friend?

Laronne watched as the elderly black man spoke to the newspaper reporter. No doubt he was telling the same story he told the television cameras—now it was well rehearsed. Spic-and-span wasn't a way to remember a woman, a mother. And why was the man making himself part of a story he knew nothing about?

"Did you know her?" the reporter asked Laronne next. "How did you know her? Was she a good employee?"

"Yes," Laronne said. "She worked for me at the library. She was the hardest working. Always on time until this week."

"How did she seem to you when you saw her last?" the reporter finally asked.

Laronne thought of what she'd heard on the television reports the night before. *Quiet. Shy. Kept to herself. Spic-and-span.*

How did she seem? Nella seemed proud and hungry and young.

"What else can you tell us about her?" the reporter asked.

LARONNE THOUGHT OF the day she showed Nella a picture of her own son, Greg.

"Robbie's gonna be a big boy like this," Nella had said.

"It happens before you know it," Laronne had replied.

"Now, they're still my little sunshines." Nella smiled. "Robbie especially is a little brown kiss."

Laronne knew the kids only from the framed photograph on Nella's desk, but she remembered that Nella always spoke about the boy special. She said he didn't talk much because he stuttered. He pointed. He nodded. Or he had his big sister say for him what he wanted to say. The girl certainly had enough words in her for all of them. Who knew what she'd grow up to be, but it would certainly be whatever she wanted; it would be written as large as the sky.

Nella rubbed the front of Laronne's picture as she handed it back. "I'm sorry. Did I get it dirty?" she asked.

"No, that's a scrape above his eye," Laronne said. "It's just a scar now, but Lord when he first came home. I think it hurt me more than him."

"That's how it is. You want to protect them."

"Funny how that happens," Laronne said. "You realize you'd do anything for them. Anything for them to be okay."

"Yes," Nella said. "I will."

LARONNE HAD ONLY one thing to say to the reporter. "That woman loved her babies, and they loved her."

The reporter wrote down what Laronne said. But Laronne could tell the reporter didn't think it made for a good story.

Laronne wanted to say something that mattered. "You have to ask the right questions," she said. "What no one's asking is: Where is the man? The boyfriend?" The reporter made a sound to encourage Laronne to keep talking. "What we need to ask is," Laronne said, "where was *he* that day?"

A black woman who had taken up on Laronne's left said, "That's right," and Laronne was in church again—testifying as she thought of Nella's boyfriend, the man with the orange hair slicked back who was nowhere to be found.

"What we need to be asking . . ." Laronne was all emotion. "Was that man up on that roof that day?"

"Amen." The black woman who had suddenly taken up on her left was her chorus.

Doug—that was his name. Funny how Laronne made him a black man in her mind when Nella first mentioned him. She wasn't sure if it was out of her own bias or a certain wish. From what Nella said, the man—Doug—didn't seem to have a real job. That could have been the reason she thought the man was black—her bias.

"A woman—no woman—would do that to her own children," Laronne said.

"Amen."

The reporter scribbled furiously on her pad.

"You go on, ask people what they saw. A woman doesn't sacrifice her babies that way. No matter what's gone wrong. She's not gonna hurt no kids. But maybe *that man* did."

And with that Laronne saw the reporter write a giant asterisk and exclamation point.

"Would you spell your name for me again?"

THAT NIGHT LARONNE couldn't sleep as it stormed outside. Her thoughts of Nella and of the boy and baby, now dead, and the girl, these things had made a bookmark inside of her.

"David," she said to her husband as she turned toward him in bed. "The sadness is coming over me again."

"I know. Come here."

Laronne moved closer and let herself feel the warmth of his arms around her shoulders and on her back, and the heat of his chest on her face.

"I can't get rid of the sadness," Laronne said.

"Well," David said, "then we'll just keep it company."

IN THE MORNING Laronne found the story on page B3. The reporter had described the courtyard, the shrine, the collection of people who prayed and whispered. There were more words to describe the after-scene than there were to describe any of the lives that were lost. The reporter used the words *pity, tragedy, shame.* No mention of *bravery, courage, love.*

But then there in black and white she read: "Police say they are continuing their investigation to rule out foul play. Witnesses indicate possible suspects . . ." Her eyes fixed on the word "Witnesses." Someone had seen what happened? What could they tell?

Rachel

It's the sound I remember. "Ma-ko-me-none," I say when the counselor at science camp asks what kind of plant that is. "That's a bearberry plant in Ojibway," I say. I read it in a book about a Native American princess who had long hair down to the ground. She saved her family by making her hair a rope and pulling them from the water.

"That's my mom's tribe," Anthony Miller says. "For real."

Then all the kids laugh, including Antoine who is supposed to be Anthony Miller's best friend. I look at Anthony Miller real hard and try to see history.

"Ooo-wah-oo-wah." Antoine is the one who does it first. He claps his hand to his mouth the way Indians on TV do. Then he sticks out his lip and makes *Ojibway* a word for the kid on *Fat Albert*. The other kids laugh harder. I don't know if it's better to have people laugh at what you are or just not understand.

Anthony Miller is handsome and has a broad nose and thick lips, and those are the black things in a person. His nose is Pop's nose. And his brownness is Aunt Loretta's. He doesn't have to have an Ojibway part that people can see for me to believe him.

Anthony Miller doesn't look sad that the other kids are laughing, because he is laughing too. He laughs along with them. And he starts to dance around. Anthony Miller always laughs.

I like Anthony Miller even though he's the one that bumps my chair. He knows I like him because Tracy told him. I don't know if that makes her my best friend ever or my enemy. I think he likes me too. He told Tracy that I should meet him before dinner at the big tree that has more than 150 rings.

We are standing under the big tree that has more than 150 rings when Anthony Miller says, "Let me tell you a secret." He pulls me closer to him than I have ever been to a boy. Then Anthony Miller kisses me on the lips. The kiss runs all the way to my middle. He kisses my hurt ear next, not knowing that it is hurt, and strokes my hair along my back. Anthony Miller makes me a princess. "All of this is a secret," he says, and I listen. "Because I really have another girl."

"Lolo," the woman says and hugs Aunt Loretta real tight while they're standing at the door.

I thought it was Grandma's friend Miss Verle coming for a visit to discuss the scripture, like she does just about every other day. Really Grandma and Miss Verle are just talking about what happened on their stories and the good things they found at the St. Vincent de Paul thrift store in the part of town where Grandma works. You can buy a whole bag of clothes for five dollars there. "White people throw some valuable stuff away," Miss Verle always says. "Throws it out like it don't even matter."

I always know when they start talking about me or white folks because they start to talk real low. Sometimes I think that I can hear better because I have one good ear. No matter how softly they whisper I can hear them. And when Miss Verle says "them titties" make me look "too growed up." I can hear her and hear Grandma agree. She means grown up, I say inside, but there are special rules for how she says things since she's from down South. I want to correct her but don't.

"Helen! It's so good to see you. Come in. What are you doing here?" Aunt Loretta says and hugs the woman again.

Helen is a tall, light-skinned-ed woman with short but straight hair. She's wearing a red silk shirt, black pants, and heels. She's almost as pretty as Aunt Loretta and has the same wide smile.

"In town visiting my family, and I saw Pam downtown yesterday. She mentioned you were back in town so I thought I'd see if your mom could help me find you."

"Well, I'm here. Living here now."

Something about the way Aunt Loretta talks sounds different to me. Maybe Aunt Loretta doesn't feel so sure.

Helen looks at me then and says: "Oh my, you and Nathan did something good here!"

"This is my niece, Rachel. Roger's daughter. She's living here with mama and me."

"Hi, Miss Helen," I say and shake her hand.

"Hi, Rachel. Aren't you a sweetie. Firm handshake. That's good home training. But call me Helen. You make me sound like some old woman with that Miss. And we aren't that old!" she says looking at Aunt Loretta.

They both laugh.

"Come in. Sit down," Aunt Loretta says. "And Rachel, go put on some water for tea."

Everything about Aunt Loretta seems real formal like Helen isn't her high school friend, but something like a queen.

From the kitchen I can hear Aunt Loretta and her friend talking—as clearly as I can hear Grandma and Miss Verle.

"You know I went to college. Just down to California. That's as far as my imagination could take me then," Helen says. "And then, you know, I loved it there. I wanted to see more. So for law school I went to Howard. I'm at a firm in D.C. So is my husband."

"That's great," Aunt Loretta says. "I knew you'd do great."

"Last I heard you and Nathan had run off and got married. You two were moving somewhere for him to play ball. And you know you hurt my feelings, right? I was supposed to be the maid of honor."

"Oh, it wasn't a special thing. We did it simple—at the courthouse."

"I bet Miss Doris was none too happy about that. She'd been wanting to fit you for a wedding gown since we were in seventh grade!"

"Mama has her own ways," Aunt Loretta says. "I think she was still glad I had a man and I didn't run off alone, for some crazy other thing."

"Bless her heart," Helen says laughing before her voice gets real soft. "Lolo, what happened with Nathan?"

"He did play ball. I loved the time we lived in New York, the museums, the galleries, the energy. I worked up the nerve to take a couple art classes too. I was working up the nerve to maybe show some pieces—like to a gallery. But then Nathan and I—it didn't work out." Aunt Loretta's voice suddenly sounds shaky and high.

"I'm sorry," Helen says.

"You know how Nathan was," Aunt Loretta says. "He kept being Nathan. He couldn't help but mess around. Aunt Loretta pauses for just a second and says in almost a whisper: "Then he didn't care what it was he was messing with. He messed around with it all—my friends, his friends' wives, and then whatever, woman or man."

"I'm sorry. I didn't mean to bring it all up."

There is a long silence, and I hope the teakettle won't suddenly blow, so I turn the heat off before the water boils.

"It's so good to see you," Aunt Loretta says. "How long are you in town?"

"A couple more days. But you know my sister's back living here now. She's trying to get the Jack and Jill back up and running. That's all you Miss Rose Festival Princess! It's time we had some more black folks in this town doing something."

I carry in the teapot and cups on a tray, and Aunt Loretta turns as if she had forgotten I was there.

"Aren't you a dear," Helen says and pats me on the shoulder. "Do it for this one here—she's a Jack and Jill girl or a Links deb if I ever saw one. Make sure she meets up with the right boys."

Aunt Loretta takes the tray from me and sets it down. "Is that something you want to do Rachel? Have a coming-out ball?"

"I don't know," I say. "Is it like a confirmation? In Denmark everyone has a confirmation when they turn fourteen. You wear a white dress like a wedding."

"Denmark?"

"My mom's from Denmark."

"That brother of yours was so fine," Helen says to Aunt Loretta. "Figures some white woman would snatch him up," she says laughing. "All those years, I was thinking I was going to be Mrs. Morse."

After Helen leaves, Aunt Loretta hardly says a word all through dinner and even when we clean up after dessert.

"Aunt Loretta, are you okay?" I ask when she comes to say good night.

"I'm fine, Rachel. Just fine."

But I can see she's not, and for the first time I think that smiling Aunt Loretta has middle layers like me. Maybe she's made herself into the new girl too.

No one except Tracy knows that when the bus lets us off at Holy Redeemer after school I meet Anthony Miller in the empty vestibule. I wait inside, up fourteen steps. And sometimes I really believe that God *is* right there behind the large oak doors, because he's sending Anthony Miller to me.

It is cold in the vestibule, and empty and dark. The only light comes from the three stained-glass windows at the vestibule's top nearly thirty feet high. The left window is a man kneeling with his hands in prayer. His eyes are open and looking up at an empty throne with a cross on top. The throne is bejeweled—that's my new favorite word. It sounds like a command and has such long sounds it could go on forever. The jewels on the throne cast triangles of red, green, and blue light on the marble steps. On the days the bus driver skips the stop before Holy Redeemer where only one student gets off, the light will be just right and we can stand on the steps in those jewels. I can see Ojibway angles to Anthony Miller's face in that light, but I don't tell him that.

In the middle window above the door is the other half of the chair and Jesus standing next to it. Jesus looks out of the corner of his eye toward the kneeling man as if he's laughing at the man for bowing to the chair. I wonder whether that happens all the time: God stands to the side wondering why we keep asking for wishes to come true from empty chairs. The window on the right is the same size as the one on the left. It's a picture of a long table with the food all gone and the chalices spilled over. But there is no spill. Maybe that is what the man in the left picture window is asking: Please don't let us be thirsty.

When Anthony Miller kisses me, I try not to sweat; I'm so happy. I don't want to drown in this feeling. I feel light the way

I did when Mor would hold me in her arms as we swam. This isn't what Grandma means when she prays for the sick to be lifted up, but maybe this is what it feels like. We kiss until the light changes; that's when people come into the church again. I like to have this secret. Anthony Miller is only for me. Inside.

MISS AMERICA IS black today, and she has blue eyes. There is a small picture on the bottom of the newspaper's front page. She doesn't look black to me. Grandma picks up two newspapers to have one extra. She is happy that a black woman is the most beautiful woman in the world. And so is the grocery store cashier. It's a new day, the grocery store cashier says. And I believe that I am supposed to be happy about it.

The grocery store clerk is dark-skinned-ed, like Grandma and Aunt Loretta. Not Grandma nor the grocery store clerk look anything like the white-looking black woman with blue eyes who is the first black Miss America.

And then I think: I could be Miss America if I got prettier.

But I am going through an awkward phase Aunt Loretta says. My hair is short and frizzy. I cut the tangles right off my tender head one night with my science-class scissors. When Grandma saw me with this short, frizzy thing no one could call a hairstyle, she said, "What done got into you to cut the hair off your head?"

I won't be all nappy anymore. That's what I said but only inside. Outside I just shrugged.

AT THE AME ZION CHURCH, when we sing holiday songs, beneath my breath I sing the Danish words. The choir is so loud no one can tell that during "Silent Night" I sing *stille* and not "still," *hellige* and not "holy." I'm glad I remember these sounds. I have learned a lot of words since I came to Grandma's. *Dis, conversate, Jheri curl.* There are a lot more. And sometimes I feel those words taking up too much space. I can't remember how to say cotton in Danish or even the word for cloud. What if you can have only so many words in you at once? What happens to the other words?

My friend Tracy sometimes makes me say Danish stuff to test me. Then she giggles and says, "It sounds like you're talking Scooby-Doo language. Like I can almost understand."

"Well I can understand what I'm saying."

"Say some more."

"Like what?"

"Like—I like kissing boys," she says.

Then we laugh because we do. Tracy likes a boy in our math class, but she says he probably likes me. His name is Jay. He has light brown hair that waves—not curls. There's a difference. And really long eyelashes like a girl doll. I think maybe he is Jewish because his last name is Stein. I told Tracy that I know Jay doesn't like me, for sure. He's white. White people don't think black people are pretty. Mostly it's because of our hair. It works different. And it smells different with more lotions in it. Also, black women are not as pretty as white women. There are exceptions—Aunt Loretta, Miss America—but not many.

FOR GRANDMA THERE'S a lot of church in Christmas. There's a lot of church for her in most things. So when

Aunt Loretta brings home the not real Christmas tree coated in fake snow, Grandma decorates it with a star on top, blue tinsel, and her angel ornaments.

Grandma unwraps her ceramic angels one by one. They all kneel in prayer with their hands clasped together. They wear white robes and white wings. Grandma wipes off each one and gives their halos a good shine. Then she sets them on the coffee table so that they look like a choir lining up to sing.

"Grandma, all of your angels are white," I say.

"Angels are angels," Grandma says.

"But they all have blue eyes and blond hair," I say. Grandma looks at her collection then really hard at me.

"Angels ain't people," she says. Then Grandma makes a humph sound and leaves the room.

The Christmas tree is the background to all of the photos Aunt Loretta takes on Christmas Day. There's the new girl opening presents; there she is saying thank you to Grandma with a big hug; she's eating the pie Grandma made special; and there she is again saying good night in a brand-new nightgown. And the tree is always right behind her with Grandma's angels and their bright white faces.

That night when I close my eyes to sleep, Grandma's angels are the only thing on my mind. The angels and me—we all line up for a song. We sing "Glade Jul." Again and again. We let ourselves sing off key. We dance around the Christmas tree. The angels flap their wings, and then I see Mor—yes, it's her. Right there in the second row. And Ariel. She's there too with her smaller halo, and she sings too. And Robbie. He looks just like himself even though he's wearing that white robe and fluffy white wings. Robbie flaps so hard he's shaking his feathers free. Small and soft and white. The other angels flap just as hard. We're in a blizzard of white. We sing all night. Until it's time for a new day.

AT SCHOOL EVERYTHING about black history you learn in one month. I already learned about most of the things in my other school. The main ones are slavery and how Lincoln made the slaves free, how there were different water fountains, and about Martin Luther King Jr. There are black women in history too—Rosa Parks, Harriet Tubman, and Phillis Wheatley. I hear the stories different now though. They make me think of the day that Pop was sad because the fastest man in the world had died, and the time that Mor and Pop said we were too young to watch the movie about slavery on TV. Whatever those things had to do with each other, I know now that they also had something to do with me.

Brick

Brick peered into several rooms before he found her. And then he stood by the door for a long while before the man in the military uniform by the girl's bed noticed him.

"You here for Rachel?" the man asked when he looked up, his voice trembling.

"Yes, sir. My name is," and he hesitated before saying, "Brick."

"Come on in. You can't hurt her."

The man wore a dark blue military uniform, tie, light blue long-sleeved shirt, polished black shoes. There were five stripes like wings on his shirt sleeve. His hat was set on the rolling table by the girl's bed.

The deep purple that was the girl's left side resembled a

birthmark. A tube jutted from her mouth. Wires and machines hung above and surrounded her bed.

"I was going to play for my girl." The man took from his pocket a silver harmonica. He put it to his lips and played a sad-sounding song.

The man played the tune once, then twice more. By the second go-through, Brick had perched himself on the chair next to the man. He closed his eyes.

"Can I try?" Brick asked when the man was done.

The man wiped the harmonica with a handkerchief.

"Hold it like this," he said and demonstrated for Brick.

Brick held the harmonica to his mouth as the man had shown him. He blew. So much breath was in him his first note sounded like a horn.

The girl's eyes opened.

Brick stepped back and knocked over the rolling table.

"I'm sorry. I'm sorry." He repeated the words until he wore them down.

The girl's eyes closed as suddenly as they had opened.

"It's okay," the man said, holding Brick. His hands were strong and calming. And then, as Brick gave a feather-light touch to press back, the man seemed to break. He took Brick in his arms and wept. When the man finally lifted his head from Brick's shoulder, he said, "She'll get better. She has to." Then he stood soldier straight and shook Brick's hand. "You can come back anytime."

BRICK VISITED THE next day again. The man was playing the same song when Brick arrived. Brick stood by the door until he was through. "Come in," the man said when he noticed Brick. "I'm going to teach you this—one note at a time."

The man's shirt was wrinkled. His scent from yesterday had doubled from heat.

The man took a flask from the inside of his uniform jacket, which hung on the chair he sat in. He drank. "Okay, this is how it goes."

BRICK VISITED THE next day again.

The man seemed to be waiting for him. He called him over to the chair by the girl's bed, hoisting him onto his lap. "What do you remember of the song?" Brick took the harmonica from the man and played an unsteady tune.

"Not bad. Not bad."

Brick played the tune again and again. The man sometimes stopped him to remind him of a forgotten note. Every few minutes the man drank from the flask, which he tucked into a duffel bag after each long sip. The man's eyes were red today and heavy-lidded. Long circles stained his sleeves, and he had a spot on the front of his untucked shirt.

The girl—half of her the color of red wine—breathed to the machine's rhythm. The man and Brick sat silently watching her for many minutes.

"She your girlfriend?" the man asked as he eyed Brick.

"Huh?"

"She your girlfriend? My daughter your girl?"

"No, sir." Brick took the question as an accusation. He wasn't guilty and said so.

"She's too young for the boys. You understand, right?"

Brick blinked. It was best to agree.

"Let me ask you something." The man paused, then coughed—the last swig from his flask had caught in his throat. "You ever been in love?"

Brick's face became a question mark.

"It's a bitch. What you'll do. What you'll need."

Rachel

There's nothing better than June because it's the end of the school year and there's nothing but summer for weeks. Except first it's Race Day. It's the end-of-the-year Olympics, and our class is Guam. Mrs. Anderson likes the way it sounds, and the other good countries are taken.

I was the fastest girl in the fifth grade. Fifth grade. That's when I ran faster than everyone except Eric Smith. The teachers called him Eric S. We called him Fast Eric. There was also Erik K. with a *k*. We called him Smart Erik. Sometimes when I used to run, I would think I could beat anybody—even Eric S. Sometimes I didn't think at all. Just ran. And it felt good.

I don't know if I can beat anyone here.

Today is Race Day and Tamika Washington looks at me. She been looking at me; she's looking at me now and started a long time ago.

But since I cut my hair Tamika Washington don't be minding me much no more. Aunt Loretta says Tamika is jealous because her hair won't grow. Now that my hair is shorter than Tamika's she calls me Afro-head, because my hair curls up any way it wants and hers is straight and flat. I don't understand why Tamika is looking at me that way.

Tamika gets the other girls to look at me that way too. Tamika has a lot of friends: Tonya, Keisha, Sierra, and even Carmen LaGuardia. I have one girlfriend and a boyfriend. But my friend is white and my boyfriend is secret. I have no black friends.

Black girls don't seem to like me. Maybe there is something dangerous about me. Aunt Loretta says there isn't. Good students aren't always going to be popular with their peers. Those are her exact words. "You make them have to work harder."

I want to be a good student. I know how to do that. I think being a good student will help me in the long run. I think of the long run, the way that Aunt Loretta says it. Me, running, down the sidewalk past the old German dairy store and Emanuel Hospital, across the Fremont Bridge, and through the hills that must lead to somewhere. Aunt Loretta wishes she had thought about the long run, had studied more, gotten a better job and a husband different than Uncle Nathan that wasn't so funny and didn't have a special kind of disease just for men who are funny like him. You can get real sad later if you don't think about the long run as open arms that will hold you.

The race starts. I run. I run faster than Tamika. And maybe I'm going as fast as Eric S. would. I run and run harder. And I cross the finish line first.

The medal ceremony is in the middle of the football field so everyone can see. I go to the center of the field. It is Carmen LaGuardia, the student class president, who gives me the blue ribbon and medal I will wear home that afternoon. I imagine how she will put the blue ribbon with the golden saucer-sized medallion around my neck. Gently, gently. Then smooth the front of my shirt with a long, soft stroke. She will take my hand and raise it in victory, and everyone will see that the beautiful Carmen LaGuardia is just like me. She is no longer one of the fifteen. And I will no longer count myself as one.

These are the first words she says to me: "Mmmh, girl. You got them boys pantin with your titties all hanging out. Don't try to steal my man with those." Tamika is second place and bends at the waist laughing. She is still bent over when Carmen LaGuardia puts the smaller medallion around her neck and then gives her a high five. I don't cry. I have the blue bottle. I make resolutions. I turn twelve next month. It's Day 223. I'm the new girl. I must be the new girl. I will fill myself with the color blue.

Roger

When Roger first met Nella, the joint was getting so hot that the windows dripped with dew. Isaac Hayes blared from four-foot Pioneer speakers, and the dance floor was full.

"First time in this joint, huh? My first time too. Just visiting my buddy Maurice—over there—I'm up from Ramstein," Roger said when he approached Nella.

Roger liked white girls, but not American white girls. They didn't do much for him, because they acted like you were supposed to be happy just because you got to rub your brown on their cream. But not these European girls—they loved the black boys they met in the bars near the American base. Roger loved them back.

He didn't wait for Nella to answer. A smile was enough invitation. And she did smile, even though it was hidden behind her hand.

"My name's Roger Morse."

"Nella Fløe."

"Nella Flow. You ready to cut loose? Do you flow when you dance?"

He could tell she didn't understand all of what he said: *joint, loose.*

"You're from here?" he asked.

"I'm Danish," she said.

"Danish, huh? Danish girl, what's it like there? In Danish-land?"

Nella laughed.

"Danish is from Denmark," she said. She was from a small town on the peninsula, Herning.

"Her-kneeing," Roger said, imitating her accent as he put a hand on her leg.

Nella laughed, but she didn't move away.

"Denmark. That's where those stories are from. The ones we read as a kid."

"Hans Christian Andersen?"

"Yeah, yeah. I used to dig that stuff as a kid."

Nella looked at him quizzically.

"Like," Roger said. "Dig is like."

"Oh."

"So what's a pretty Danish girl doing here?" he asked.

"Practicing my English. Then I am going back home to go to school," Nella said.

Roger smiled wide. "I can teach you some language," he said and scooted closer to Nella, putting his arm around her. She touched her hand to his leg.

They danced that night. They kissed. Roger recited for Nella some Shakespeare he learned from a Vincent Price album. That seduced a girl easy. Never underestimate the appeal of a black boy speaking in tongues. That was Roger's personal style.

They kissed some more. And that night Roger couldn't help but make love to that shy white girl who came from a little town in a little country he knew nothing about—except that in her country's stories, wishes came true.

Rachel

Aunt Loretta has taken me for the first time to see the Multnomah Falls, beautiful waterfalls about one hour away from Grandma's. Only they're not moving. Waterfall after waterfall is frozen in midstream—giant icicles—stuck in a going down way.

The biggest waterfall is as tall as a cathedral. We walk up the wooden trail steps as high as we can. The wind tickles up the back of my neck even though I am wearing a hat and am wrapped up with a scarf so that you can only see my eyes. It's so cold even Aunt Loretta's cheeks are red. "That Indian's showing up in you," Drew says and kisses her cheek with his frozen breath.

We stand before the waterfall like we are in church. Drew, Aunt Loretta, and me. We stand on the little wooden bridge high above the water and hold our hands together as we watch nothing. The water's not moving.

Maybe eight other people are standing nearby watching the nonmoving water not move.

There are no black people in Nature today. Only us.

The wind catches me at the ankles now. My socks have fallen on the climb up the stairs to this lookout point.

"No way we could get Miss Doris up to see this," Drew says.

"There's no way my mama wants to be out in the thick of cold climbing up stairs to see anything but the Lord himself," Aunt Loretta says. "But if she did . . ."

Aunt Loretta doesn't finish what she's saying. She stares out at the falls and moves her hands in the air like she can measure what she is seeing. Like she's framing it with her hands.

"You about done with this cold, Rachel?" Drew asks.

"Yes, sir."

Aunt Loretta is leaning on the rail, looking at the waterfall now. She's hypnotized. I think she is crying.

Drew sees that she is crying too.

Aunt Loretta cries without sound, but I can see a shudder go through her. Is it the cold wind? Drew is saying something to her. I hear in only half volume. The wind is in my good ear, and in the other a thrumming, a hum.

"I want to be that girl again," is all I can hear of what Aunt Loretta says. Drew seems to know what she means. He leans into her, but I move away. I don't want hands on me.

I take small steps backing off the bridge. I walk slowly and carefully. What I'm scared of I can't explain. It's the look in

Aunt Loretta's eyes, the way her voice sounds small and hurt. Maybe she's measured a long icy fall.

When I finally get off the bridge, I see that Drew is still holding Aunt Loretta. But then suddenly she pushes him away to stand up straight again.

By the time we are sitting in the lodge drinking hot cocoa, Aunt Loretta doesn't look like herself, but she doesn't look broken. We laugh about Drew losing his hat. A strong wind stole it. He grabbed for it, but it was already gone, flying down toward the frozen stream below. We laugh about the woman who said my eyes were pretty but then looked at Aunt Loretta and Drew real funny. "Maybe she thought I was stolen," I say and laugh. But I think what a family is shouldn't be so hard to see. It should be the one thing people know just by looking at you.

"Now, if I didn't have this mustache, we'd basically be twins you and me," Drew says. I laugh, but Aunt Loretta doesn't join in. Aunt Loretta just smiles.

AUNT LORETTA SEES new after the day at the falls. Old things, throwaway things, leftover things, she sees them new and different and worthy. She makes Grandma save the bags from her morning tea on a plate by the toaster oven. She wants my old crayons—the ones that are broken or stubby nubs. She collects leaves from the dying flowers in Grandma's garden. She saves pebbles and wrappers and peels. And she makes things with them.

Aunt Loretta has always decorated herself. Now she decorates the house. She has replaced the brown-green swirls on the couch with an African brown fabric that has pictures of leopards and zebras and elephants. Next to the porcelain figures of kings and queens, she's placed a statue of an Igbo goddess. The goddess means life and fertility and nobility. Aunt Loretta is teaching me about African things. African can mean a lot of things and it's important to be specific. Aunt Loretta has never been to Africa but wants to go one day.

On the walls she's hung a photograph of an old Asian man with a straw hat, and one of a Masai man, a certain kind of African man, in a bright yellow tunic. Grandma doesn't like any of these things. She doesn't want her house "lookin so African." She likes things respectable, she says. She fusses but she doesn't take down the pictures or the statues. Almost every day there is something new: a new mask or trinket or something hanging on the wall.

Grandma tut-tuts when she sees Aunt Loretta has set up an easel in her bedroom. After the day at the falls, Aunt Loretta dug out an easel, paints, and a paint cloth from the basement trunks. "Don't be makin a mess," Grandma says. "You never careful with the mess that makes."

Grandma is worried about neatness and order and doesn't have time for messy things. She doesn't think Aunt Loretta should either. A lizard is not going to be interested in a woman with paint underneath her nails, or a woman smelling of chemicals instead of peaches and white soap.

Aunt Loretta paints every day now. She paints from memory at first. Every day she makes a new painting of a waterfall, moving or not moving. She calls them *Untitled 1, Untitled 2,* and so on, until she gets to number 15. She names the next ones *Figure by the Falls, Woman on Bridge by the Falls, The Dream by the Falls*. I make up better titles for them, but she doesn't use them. But then she uses me.

She wants to do my profile, and I am supposed to look down. I don't know how to sit still. I notice I am making the same face as the statue on the mantel.

"Funny, you have that same wrinkle your dad had."

"Really?"

"Your dad was the most handsome man. I think some of my friends were my friends just so they could be near to him."

"But my dad was also the smartest," I say without a question mark, because this is how I remember him.

"He sure couldn't spell, but that's supposed to be a sign of genius. Double consonants. Those always got him. He'd make them double when they shouldn't be and vice versa."

Aunt Loretta doesn't talk much while she paints, but I ask her anyway, "Did he like any of your friends? Like Helen."

Aunt Loretta laughs. "I suppose so. There was Helen. A couple more."

"How did they look?" I ask. And for some reason what I mean is: Did they look like Mor? Or did they look like me? "Were they all light-skinned-ed?" I ask.

"Light-skinned," she says. "It's light-skinned, and the answer is . . . maybe. I never thought about it."

"Aunt Loretta, when do you think he'll come back to get me?"

She doesn't answer the question I ask. Instead she says, "He came to the hospital, Rachel." Suddenly the hum of Grandma's story playing in the next room isn't the loudest thing in the house. "Those days, those first days," she continues, "he held your hand and stroked your hair smooth."

"But then he went on the mission? I don't remember."

"You were very, very sick."

"I almost died."

"But you didn't."

"When he finishes the mission, he'll come back," I say.

"Rachel, you know we don't know. We don't know how long the things he's got to do could take."

"Could he tell us?"

"No, my sweet, I'm afraid—he probably doesn't know either."

Aunt Loretta says "hush" after that but in a gentle way when she can tell I want to ask more. I have to be still for her to paint me. And for some reason I think about feeling lonely, right here in front of her. And I think about the things that maybe made Pop feel alone, right in front of us, his family. No one knew how to cut his hair—he had tight black curls like other black people. And maybe he even had ash on his elbows and knees sometimes. He never told us he was black. He never told us that we were.

"The light's not right," Aunt Loretta says.

Or I am a bad model, I think. There is something hidden about me that she can't quite paint, Aunt Loretta says, but the word she uses is one of the big words I've learned: *elusive*.

AUNT LORETTA STOPS painting people and makes paintings of animals. They look like the African animals on the couch. But they are not the same, Aunt Loretta tells me. I have never heard of a quagga or a thylacine or a moa. And even when Aunt Loretta tells me what they are, they still look like zebras and tigers and ostriches. She says these animals are different. They are extinct.

She paints these animals against a blue or red backdrop that looks like the sky or a burning fire. In her paintings the animals are in motion, in the air, doing backflips and somersaults and high dives. I imagine them springing off that wooden bridge that stretches above the falls. I cannot imagine them land.

Aunt Loretta says they are part of a series she calls Secrets of Extinction. I think about what those secrets may be. And I think about who keeps the secret if really you're the last one. I think maybe she should call them Moments of Extinction. Because she's painting what makes them move toward the end. It's a funny thing to think about: moving toward extinction. And I think of how maybe I'm already extinct in a strange way—there's no way to make another me: at least I can't do it. But that doesn't matter anyway because I never want to have kids.

Brick

Brick visited the next day again.

He played the song two notes short of good, the man said with a smile. "You hear how you're making a song out of what's just a whistle. Like a bird," the man said.

"Yes," Brick said.

The two sat quietly for a long time before Brick asked, "Sir, what do you do?"

"I'm a mapmaker."

"Oh."

"I map out where they can bomb the commies, when the time is right."

"Really?" Brick's eyes were wide. "Who?"

"Our guys. They go up in the big planes and find the targets with my maps."

"How?"

"You know I'm not supposed to tell you any of this. It's classified. You know what that means?"

"Huh-uh."

"Secret. Means it's secret. Folks think we're not at war— cause we're outta Nam. But we're always at war. Long as those commies are there, we're gonna find a way to get them. When the time's right, we're gonna get them. Let me show you."

The man stood and moved the chair away from the girl's bed. "We'll make you the pilot," the man said. "And I'll call you Charles."

He motioned for Brick to sit and handed him a chart from the rolling table. He put his hat on Brick's head.

"Pretend that chart's the map I made," the man said, and he took a long sip from his flask and set it beneath the chair. Then he extended his hand to Brick, his fingers slightly bent as if he was holding something.

The boy took from the man what was only air, but Brick was careful to mimic the shape of his hand. In his hand, the man explained, Brick held a walkie-talkie. The man had one too.

With the words "take off," the man sent the boy flying high above the German air base, over water and mountains, over Soviet enemy ground. "Do you see the target?" he asked.

The boy consulted his map. "Yes, sir."

"Shoot, anytime."

Brick let go of the controls and pushed the button.

The man made the sound of an exploding bomb in a stage whisper.

"Okay, got it!" Brick raised his arms for victory.

"No, no, no . . . you say something like . . . the Eagle has landed. Remember! It's classified. It's all secret. It has to be in code," the man said.

"The Eagle has landed."

"We copy you. Come on back down," the man said. He drank again from the flask.

Brick smiled. Mission accomplished. The alarm bells suddenly went off as they often did, and a nurse entered the room to check.

The nurse, seeing the boy's stricken face, said, "Don't worry. If it does that, everything's working well."

The man adjusted his hat on the boy's head. He saluted him.

"Want to be like your daddy, huh?" the nurse asked and turned to check on the girl.

"Okay, now what do you want to play?" the man asked after the nurse had left the room. The flask was in his hand again. He had an unlit cigarette in his mouth. Brick shrugged. He was holding onto the walkie-talkie, the chart map, the feeling of being worthy of a salute.

"Well. What?" Another long drink.

"I don't know." Brick didn't know games.

"Hide and seek. You want to play hide and seek?" the man said like a tickle.

Brick laughed.

"Hide and seek? Hide and seek?" The man did tickle him, lassoing Brick at the waist with heavy arms. Brick squealed. He thought he had stopped his body from needing this—touch that equaled joy. But then the tickles became jabs. The man's hold was not a lasso but a noose.

"Let me tell you something, Charles. I tried to find you. I did try!"

The man had a sad faraway look in his eyes. Brick was shaking.

"You okay? I didn't mean that, okay?" the man said. Suddenly he was weeping again, and Brick moved away, across the room.

He looked at the man from the safety of the doorway. "I know."

"Going outside," Brick called to his mother the next day. He walked downstairs. The wind thumped the courtyard seesaw against the ground again and again.

Brick sat on a swing wet from the morning rain. He pushed hard enough to swing past the puddle below him, but he let his feet drag through the mud just because he was big enough now to reach. He imagined himself back in the cockpit, each splash through the puddle a direct hit on enemy ground.

"The Eagle has landed. The Eagle has landed. The Eagle has landed." But it wasn't the same.

Brick swung back and forth slowly to a stop. His reflection waved in the muddy puddle beneath him. And then the water suddenly splashed.

"What you tell them, Shorty?"

Brick was silent and shaking.

"Huh?" said the man, grabbing his arm. Brick hadn't seen the man who raised pigeons on the roof in weeks. Brick had stopped visiting him when the man's large ring bruised Brick's thigh. He didn't want to be called Shorty, and he didn't want the man to call him pretty. Besides, Brick liked a fancier bird than a pigeon.

"You told them I was up there? If I wanted to I could fix your pretty little ass."

Brick had no words.

"Look, yo. Only a crazy bitch would kill her kids. That bitch looked crazy for real. I ain't no criminal. The cops let all my pigeons go. They smashed the cages. You know how much money I lost because of your shit, Shorty?"

Brick stayed silent.

"Now you got nothing to say, huh?" The man held his arm tighter, and Brick could feel the ring press into his flesh. "Yo, Shorty. Anybody ask again you tell them the truth. Tell them what I'm telling you. I didn't see nothing. Yeah, I was on that roof scoping out new places for my cages. And maybe I'm the one who broke the lock. But that was months ago, and that crazy bitch was gonna jump anyhow."

Muddy and wet, Brick sat still even after the pigeon man let him go. He sat still even after the pigeon man walked away. Since the moment Brick said his new name he had not thought of the story that created it. He thought of it now.

Roger

"I hope she's gonna get better." The boy's voice startled him awake. Roger had been sleeping with his head bent over Rachel's bed. He looked up and then stood and saluted the boy.

"How's it going?" Roger ushered Brick into the room. The mud was still wet on the boy's jeans.

"Little wet outside, huh?" Roger said. "Here." He took his jacket from the back of the chair and wrapped it around Brick like a cape. "Better?"

Roger wanted to erase yesterday. He wanted to hug the boy, but instead he patted his arm and said, "They say she's doing better."

"Maybe it's the song that's making her better," Brick said.

Roger swallowed audibly and turned away.

"Sir?" Brick asked.

Roger's stare into space was unbroken.

"I didn't see a man," Brick said.

"What? Where?"

"On the roof." Brick took from his pocket the newspaper folded in neat squares. He handed it to Roger, who read only as far as the headline.

"I don't want to read that shit." Roger thrust the paper back at Brick.

"I said I saw a man," Brick said. "But I didn't. But I think maybe there was a man there."

"I don't give a good goddamn what you think," Roger said. "You a detective now? You think some man did it? Maybe you did it. Maybe I did it. Maybe I was the man. The police came here asking me the same shit. You know what I care about?" He paused. "I care about my little girl getting better—if she gets out of here—keeping her safe from everything. Including me."

ROGER AND NELLA held their wedding on a Saturday at a brick red Lutheran church in her Danish hometown, where it was legal for coloreds and whites to marry. Not much later they had a son. Charles. Roger felt like he'd done something. Taken hold of something in the world even if it wasn't himself. He loved that boy. But the Little Man, as Roger called him, was broken. There was nothing exactly wrong with him. Ten fingers. Ten toes. He had the necessary parts and his mind was alert. But he was always sick. His stomach hurt. His nose bled without reason. His palms were always sweaty since he ran three degrees hotter than everyone else. And his eyes had the dark circles of a thirty-five-year-old man.

At first Roger thought he could talk Little Man into being stronger. "Wasn't it just you and the goose?" He held Little Man on his lap.

"N-n-no, Pop," Little Man would say, pretending to struggle to get away.

"Now, you don't even remember being there, do you? I remember. I remember that night you were born. Your mother was eating and drinking like no tomorrow. You see she never lost those pounds you put on her, don't you? You're the one gave your mama a nice black girl's ass."

"Roger? What are you saying?" Nella would call to "the boys" from the kitchen, her accent still heavy.

"Yeah, now you, Little Man, you stronger than you think. Now, as I recall, it was you or that goose your mother was eating. So you came right on out. Feet first."

"N-n-no, Pop," Little Man would giggle and try to tickle Roger at the waist.

"Now, you remember. You're a Morse. The Morse men are a strong bunch." Roger would pick up Little Man then and hold him in the air, jostling him.

"Put me down. P-p-put me down." Little Man would laugh.

"Roger, stop the horseplaying. His nose will start to bleed again."

"Will it Little Man? Will it?" Roger would toss Little Man into the air a bit higher each time he asked.

Little Man would laugh hysterically until Nella came into the room to stop it. Roger thought if he could will some strength into that small body, Little Man would overcome the nose-bleeds, and the colds and stomach pains that no doctor could ever cure. But Roger grew tired of Little Man being sick, of Little Man's sickness. Roger got tired of being careful, of seeing how weak his son really was. Roger would beat him when his nose bled. His hands would twist the tender yellow skin on his son's arm. Roger would use his military voice. "Stop that. Boy, you better quit." He loved that boy. He could kill him.

ROGER TOLD BRICK that in the seventies the best thing to be was black. The white people thought you had moves. They thought you knew music better and deeper than anybody else.

As the only black boy in a family of Danes—and because he got the discount on liquor with his military ID—Roger was always the center of the party. They'd play some Stevie Wonder, drink some beer, drink some Seagram's, and then some schnapps to top off the night.

That's how they spent all their holidays. Roger, Nella and the boy would drive north to Denmark to see her sister's family, or her sister's family would come visit them on base in Germany. This visit Nella's sister, Solvej came without her husband, a seaman.

"Watch out now, Nella," Roger said. "We gonna have to move tonight." Roger had never moved so good. Go on, Stevie, sing! Roger loved the harmonica interludes. He put his hands to his mouth like he was holding one.

Roger moved. He danced—and damn if he didn't start to sing too. Solvej joined in. She was a choir girl and a woman without her man around. She was cutting loose.

Roger's duet and slow dance with Solvej ended the night. But then there was the kiss good-night that lasted a little too long. It was the first time Roger had heard Nella raise her voice. She called her own sister a whore. It was also the first time Roger hit a woman—really. No, really. He didn't know how it happened. But Nella fell into her sister's arms crying, and she left with her sister. Roger was silent and drunk and watched them go.

Roger grabbed a cigarette and sat down. "My little Danish girl will come back. Won't she? Won't she, Little Man?" he said. Little Man stood behind the couch.

"Come here, boy," Roger used his cotton voice. But Little Man just stood there. "Boy, I said come here!" Roger's voice was all gravel. With that the boy sat by his father, made his father's arm around him not a noose but a wing. "We just gonna wait. My little Danish girl will come home soon. She'll come home."

It was late, so late and the music was gone. The man and the boy fell asleep together on the couch, waiting, the cigarette still lit in Roger's hand. Burning.

Roger didn't know how much time had passed when he woke coughing from the fire's smoke. Where was Little Man? He'd wriggled out from Roger's hold. Roger kept yelling into the flames. Little Man was small for his age. He could hide good. He could hide anywhere. Where was he?

"Come out, come out, wherever you are." The fire licked through the walls and inhaled the back of the wooden house in a quick blaze. Little Man was nowhere to be found, Roger told Brick. Still, he kept screaming his son's name into the flames.

"NOOO!" ROGER SCREAMED as if he were reliving that night.

The nurse rushed in, faster than she did when the alarms would ring. She checked the tubes and looked at the lines on the monitor above the bed. "What's the matter?"

Roger was holding the flask in his hand and looked at her blankly, unsteady on his feet.

"I'm sorry, sir, you'll have to go now," the nurse said. "You'll have to go."

Roger stuffed the flask, now empty, in his duffel bag and placed his hat on his head. He put on the jacket that was keeping the boy warm and lifted the bag to his shoulder. Roger paused for a moment before the boy, then handed him the harmonica.

"This is for you, a gift."

He turned and kissed Rachel's forehead.

"You tell her," he said, pointing a finger at the boy like it was a gun. "She'll want to know that story. Tell her what she never knew. She needs to understand. Her mother and me, we wanted to be together again. Had to be after Charles. No one else could of understood. That hole inside. Nella and me, we made a promise. We were gonna make a family . . . safe. Now that promise's broke. When Nella left with the kids in May . . . three months they'd been gone. Now they're gone forever. Tell Rachel—," he paused. "Tell Rachel now I'm sure she'll be safe."

Rachel

Grandma wants me in the church choir so I won't be runnin the streets. Someone shot through the glass at the Wonder Bread factory store two weeks ago. It happened on a Friday night. On the news they said gang members did it. Not gangs on TV but real gangs from California. Hearing that must have scared Grandma because that's when she said I couldn't be out alone after dark—not even for school activities. At first when she said that, I thought she had learned about the secret Anthony Miller and kissing in the vestibule. But it's been almost a year since the last time. Now Anthony Miller's going with another girl. But if he said he wanted to meet me there again, I would.

I don't fuss with Grandma about going to church. I say I'll put on the yellow dress. "And the SHOES to MATCH,"

Grandma says, making her capitals. She found the dress at the Saint Vincent de Paul thrift store with a fifty-cent price tag and a new price tag too. It doesn't fit so well around my old beige bra, but with a sweater over the top I think Grandma will like it fine. That's her best way of liking things.

If you ask me I would say that mostly I don't look like myself when I wear church finery. Or feel like a self that makes any sense. And today my scalp itches because Grandma made me go to the hairdresser to get me looking more respectable. "None of those people want to see a pickaninny in they church," Grandma said. She is glad that my hair has grown out again. I can't say that I don't like the way my hair looks. It's straight now—straight like Mor's hair for the first time ever. And it's long enough for me to move it off my shoulder with a swish. But the hairdresser let the relaxer set too long and burned a few spots on my scalp and burned my left ear with the blow-dryer's hot metal tip. And I am still tender-headed.

Two weeks ago Monday was my first day as a straight-haired girl.

Wearing my hair down and straight is one reason that the girls who hang out in the bathroom want to beat me up. They say: You better watch out or I'll snatch you bald-headed.

Is that a weave?

You think you so cute tossin that hair around.

The truth is I never toss it. I do like to pull it back like the Bionic Woman did on TV. Two fingers pulling straight back at the top of my head to show off my ears. And I am glad that there are no tangles, no naps, and no kitchen at the back of my head anymore.

But people look at me differently. I don't look just different or scary or undefinable: I look pretty. That pretty is what was Mor's: my eyes, now my straight hair. People act different around me too. Mr. Barucci, my science teacher, said something real nice. He said I looked very beautiful, a pure masterpiece. I smiled a no-teeth smile and he said, "Makes those eyes more startling to look at." And he put his fingers to his lips and made a kiss he threw in the air. "Bella!"

AUNT LORETTA AND DREW have stopped by to say hi before they go to play tennis. Aunt Loretta moved into Drew's apartment a few months ago. I wish she had taken me too. Aunt Loretta comes to visit at least twice a week, but every time she comes Grandma asks when the wedding is.

"I'm working on that lizard now," she says to Grandma in a fake whisper, leaning over to kiss her good-bye on the cheek, and points at Drew.

"He a rooster," Grandma says.

"A rooster?" Aunt Loretta laughs.

"That's the kind of lizard that take care of you," Grandma says and makes her teeth click.

Aunt Loretta's hand is on the door, and I can see all the good that will be her day. I can't wait to go where I want to go without people (Grandma) studying me. I want to walk out on a Sunday morning with my boyfriend next to me, with everybody seeing I have things to do. I start high school this year, and I'm going to get all As and think about the long run. And when I'm seventeen I'm going to go to college and then see the world. I guess I'll be someone like Aunt Loretta. Aunt Loretta is a black woman—the kind of woman I will be.

Aunt Loretta walks out the front door slowly, and I see her red red nails and her sparkly engagement ring. Grandma wasn't right. There is paint beneath Aunt Loretta's fingernails, and it doesn't matter.

Aunt Loretta is backing out the door with her tennis bag over her arm and Drew is right behind her and that light is still in her, turned on. Grandma tut-tuts because the lizard hasn't opened the door for her daughter. Aunt Loretta pauses at the threshold—she's about to go on stage. "I'm sorry you can't go with me today, sweet," Aunt Loretta says like I am a candy. It is gentle the way she says it. I mean, the way she says it sounds like a warm lake breeze. And behind the words I hear: I'll be by again real soon.

DEACON JAMES ALWAYS makes it a point to talk to Grandma at services. Deacon James is a man about Grandma's age, with no hair. He is the only deacon in the AME Zion Church with no wife even though there are a lot of women without husbands. That makes him a popular man.

Sometimes he sits next to us during the service. Today Deacon James holds Grandma's hand high in the air and makes her twirl around when he sees her.

"Miss Doris," he says, which makes Grandma bat her eyes, "you sure are lookin fine for our services today." Grandma crosses her left foot in front of her and puts her hand on her hat, posing, so Deacon James can have a picture of her in his mind. "Deacon James," she says, "I'm feeling good."

"And how's this precious young thing?"

Today I am precious and young, and last week I was sweet and shy. Deacon James cannot remember my name. Heather, Wendy, Holly he's called me over the last few months since I started going to the AME Zion Church to make Grandma happy. Deacon James, like most of the folks Grandma's age, comes from the South—North Carolina to be exact, just across the bridge from Wilsonville—and he has no history of Rachels. I am okay with precious and sweet.

Deacon James sits next to us during the service, and I know I must pay attention. It is like sitting next to the principal during a school assembly.

We stand. We sit. We sing. We sing and I only pretend sing. I can't make those big sounds that Grandma can make, or the smooth high sounds the girl who looks like Tamika can make when she does her solos. We stand and sit. And all the time, if I keep my mouth going, no one notices that no sound is coming through my lips.

I think I see Deacon James touch Grandma's knee during "His Eye Is on the Sparrow." During the next hymn he touches a little bit up her thigh. Grandma doesn't seem to notice, or she doesn't seem to mind, or she doesn't want to be impolite.

The Gospel is usually loud and has a lot of soul to it. It makes you sway, clap, almost dance. I love these big sounds in the small church. Why didn't I know about the Gospel before?

Mor used to be in a choir. It was a Danish choir and she

never learned how to do the Gospel like we do here at the AME Zion Church. The Gospel has style.

I AM AT church listening to the Gospel when never careful Aunt Loretta trips on her shoelace in a broken patch of Irving Park's public court and lands on a piece of glass no one has seen, making it love-thirty. And she's the one who's down. She cuts her face. "Oh good Lord," Grandma says, "she cut her face."

"At least she didn't poke out an eye," I say, trying to calm Grandma. But the only picture in my mind is of Aunt Loretta, her beautiful smile with a jagged slice in it and two long sewing stitches holding the sides together. And her hands covering up her smile, so she won't make Grandma mad looking at the now ugly ex–Rose Festival princess.

GRANDMA WON'T LET me go to the hospital. She says it is "too much." A young girl doesn't need to see such things. "And Loretta don't need to be exercised so." Oh, she has so many reasons. That evening I sit and pray. Not knowing how. I will lift her up.

I SNEAK UP to the hospital with Drew's help. I haven't seen Aunt Loretta in two months. Her face has a ragged scar, but that's not what's wrong, Grandma explains. They gave her medicine, and the medicine done made her sick. It's burned the outside of her and the inside and made her bleed. Her skin has come off in giant patches and sheets. I think Grandma has misunderstood. She doesn't understand the sophisticated things too well. But I hear her talking to the nurses on the phone and every day to Drew in the kitchen, and he says, "Don't be mad Mrs. Morse. They couldn't know any better. Sometimes it just happens—an antibiotic can go wrong in somebody. They were trying to help." I think of the crooked seam in Aunt Loretta's face. I think: Will Drew still love Aunt Loretta?

Drew drives me to the hospital and tells me Aunt Loretta's room number. "You know I can be late for work if you want me to go with you," he says as I get out of the car. "I can do it by myself. I'm used to hospitals," I say and wave good-bye.

Aunt Loretta is in the same hospital I went to when I first came. The nurse tells me to put on gloves, a gown, and a mask. But first wash my hands. There is a small mirror above the sink. I want to look pleasing and I practice my smile. And the way I will say "I love you" without staring at the way her face is stitched together with thread. I wash my hands and put on the gloves and gown.

"And the mask, honey. Don't forget," the nurse says.

The hospital smells stop at the door. Then it is all pink and soap and toothpaste. I can smell through the mask: It's Aunt Loretta.

But maybe I am just making this up. This room has a bare tile floor and machines on rolling poles. There are tubes that run from the machines to under Aunt Loretta's bed sheet. And there is a tube in her mouth that keeps away her smile.

I am happy that Aunt Loretta is asleep so she does not see me cry. I am happy that I am wearing this mask because my well-rehearsed smile is gone. And I can't make up the pink and the smell of soap and toothpaste anymore. The thread holding her face together has sticky brown blood on it. Her face is swollen and so are her tiny arms. The room is filled with beeps and the machine's sound for breathing.

"You okay, honey?" the nurse asks when she comes in and writes down the numbers from the machine above Aunt Loretta's bed.

"Yes, ma'am."

"Just have to give her all the love you have. That's what'll get her better. Her temperature's coming down. See that number there," and she points to the machine with three lines, "that's a good sign."

We are looking for signs because Aunt Loretta can't talk and medicine can't help her. It is the medicine that made her sick.

The nurse goes away carrying a tube of something that looks like blood from the table by Aunt Loretta's bed. Where Aunt Loretta's skin is coming off are giant white patches where she used to be brown. I make the whiteness beautiful. Not hot and raw. Like it looks now. Like giant burns. Now she will be the color of the porcelain figures in Grandma's cupboard, special. She will have the perfect color for jewels and long gloves and worship.

There is a way that people die. They get sick or they go away. It's not like shutting a door, or opening one, like Aunt Loretta did that last Sunday morning I saw her with her light on.

Laronne

As Laronne opened the apartment door, stale heat escaped and dried out her eyes. The apartment's only light came from the two living room windows. The electricity had been shut off.

It would be easy to box up what was left in the apartment. Most of their clothes were in opened suitcases, which lined the far wall along with dozens of cardboard moving boxes.

Laronne stripped the sheets from the couch. It was where Nella must have slept, like a guest in her own home.

Laronne packed up the bedding from the bassinet, the towels, the silverware, the handful of pots above the stove, and the dishes that didn't have chips.

In the bathroom medicine cabinet, she found on the top shelf shaving cream and beneath it a rusty ring, a drugstore aftershave, and Mitchum cologne. She threw the boyfriend's things away. She cleared the other shelves with a swipe of her hand, not registering who belonged to a certain toothbrush or which one's brush this might be. Laronne scrubbed the bathtub, the toilet, and the mirror with silver flakes on the edges. She wiped the cabinets, the rusty ring from the top shelf. She cleaned the floor. She cleaned each room this way. She cleaned as if it were her religion. When she was done, she was a white clean scent.

It was in the front closet where Laronne found a tote bag stuffed with papers and two hardbound journals, both filled with Nella's handwriting. Nella had scribbled addresses, grocery lists, math problems and proofs, doodles and to-do lists diagonally and haphazardly and without any logic Laronne could discern. Laronne wondered whether it was all written in English, some of the handwriting was so difficult to read.

In an entry dated two weeks before the accident, Laronne read: "He was drinking with his friend when he knows alcohol's not allowed in the house. He didn't know I had come home."

A whole section of doodling followed that, and there was a coffee ring on the left-hand side of the page. Maybe Nella had walked away from the journal. Fed the baby. Gone to bed. Not all the pages were dated. Some entries looked as if Nella had gone back to fill in new thoughts on her first impressions like she was grading herself. In blue or red ink in the margins, she had written: "wrong," "lied," "stupid," or "naive."

And though Laronne wasn't sure that it was the last entry Nella had made, on the last page of one journal she read: "They're mine. If people can't see it, how can I keep them safe?"

The spines of the two journals were marked 31 and 32. She searched through the boxes to see whether she could find more. She found numbers 10 through 15 in one box, 21 and 22 in another. She found, in all, twenty-nine journals scattered throughout a dozen boxes. Laronne stacked the journals in order. Then she read from the first page of the oldest journal dated two years ago: "This is Day 1. My first day with no drink. I hope I can keep counting to forever."

AS LARONNE LEFT Nella's apartment, she heard music. It sounded like a child practicing either in the apartment above or below. She closed the apartment door and saw a boy, the boy who had held vigil at the shrine. He was seated on the stairs one flight up. In his hands he held a harmonica.

"What's that you got there?" she asked.

The boy held the harmonica in the air to show her.

"That's pretty neat."

He shrugged.

"What are you playing?"

"Nothing," he said.

The boy walked down five stairs to the landing where Laronne stood. He was eye level to her middle.

"You live here?"

He nodded.

"Did you know . . ." She tilted her head toward the door, 6D.

The boy fidgeted and then answered, "We weren't friends." He turned and ran down the stairs. Laronne followed him and caught his eye again before he closed his apartment door.

"Hey," she said.

The boy hesitated long enough for Laronne's hand to reach the knob.

He opened the door wider.

"Hey," she said again. "You didn't tell me your name."

"Jam—," he started. "Brick."

"Rick?"

"Brick Thomas."

"Hi, Brick Thomas. Your mom home?"

He shook his head yes, then no.

"Your mama coming back soon?"

"Yeah."

"Was that you? In the newspaper?"

"Yes, ma'am."

"Did you see what happened?"

"Ma'am?"

"They say there might have been a man. Up there. Did you see him too?"

He stared at her blankly.

"On the roof that day while you were playing? Outside?"

Brick shrugged.

"What did he look like? Baby, if you know something. You should tell," Laronne said. "You know, stuff we keep inside— that's what makes it . . ."

She started over. "Here," she said, "I'm Laronne. Here's my number and my address. I live not too far away. I make some fried chicken like nobody's business. Your mama let you come over for some fried chicken?"

"Uh-huh."

Laronne handed Brick the piece of paper she'd scribbled on. "Okay, now you be sure to call. Laronne will make you some good home cooking."

"Yes, ma'am," he said as he closed the door.

THAT EVENING, WHEN Laronne claimed the title Auntie at the hospital, the nurses directed her to Rachel's room.

It had been more than a week since the accident, and the girl was beginning to heal. The deep purple bruise that was her left side was a bluish red. The nurse had washed Rachel's hair, and the soft fuzzy brown curls made a halo around her face.

Rachel was sleeping, and had been sleeping, because of the medicines she'd been given. The monitors and ventilator hummed. The doctors said it would take time, but she would probably make a full recovery—how lucky she was that her fall had been cushioned.

Laronne brought presents: a balloon, a teddy bear, a puzzle of a stallion running across an open plain. And she'd brought a book of fairy tales, stories with happy endings, as well as two boxes of Rachel's belongings that she had packed up from her room.

Laronne watched the sleeping girl sleep.

Rachel's grandmother was coming soon, a nurse told her. As soon as she was strong enough, they would fly the girl to a hospital in the grandmother's northwestern town.

"Her daddy left. The men, they can't handle nothing," the nurse said.

"Her father? He was here?"

"The drunk fool. He scared the mess out of Angela the

other day when he started yelling. She told him to get out. Ain't come back since," the nurse continued. "You should stop by, when the grandmother gets here. You're the only one who really knows anything. To tell her."

When the nurse walked away Laronne thought: But I don't know anything to tell her — at all.

Laronne sat again next to Rachel's bed and watched the machine breathe for her.

Laronne had questions, not answers. The answers might be in Nella's journals, but Laronne couldn't be sure. We lie to ourselves in many ways; we write down only what we want to understand and what we want to see. Laronne had many questions from just the few entries she'd read. Who was Charles? What was it that broke Nella? Had it been a thought and then a plan? These were questions that might answer why. But if Rachel was to live with a question about what happened, wouldn't it be easier to live with the question who? So without a second thought, Laronne stuffed into the box of Rachel's belongings the newspaper article. It was something Laronne owed Nella — she could give a mother back to her girl.

Nella

Day 744. There cannot be enough time to pack out all the boxes. Rachel and Robbie are mad they cannot play outside. They know *pas på* they tell me. But it is not safe for them playing outside in this new place when I work. They have TV. And in four weeks school begins. We can go to the park on the weekend. And I made a promise for a trip to the amusement park before school. Rachel did smile. That does not happen so much in being here. She does not talk when Doug is here. Robbie grew almost four centimeters and Rachel two centimeters. They hope they are high enough for any big rides this year. The job I have is good. The people are nice. My boss too. She has a handsome son. He looks like what maybe Robbie will look like. And in all that I forgot Charles birthday. It was two days ago. I miss him as much as ever. These two I will keep safe. I promise. I know it is hard to come here and they have no friends. I kiss Rachel in bed at night and I see her frown like I did anything wrong. She misses her dad. I kiss Robbie's forehead *god nat,* I tell him no bad dreams. It does not help. Like he has Charles memories. Like his, his twin. When school begins, it will be better. Ariel is fine and growing. She is sleeping mostly. Doug is not home. I hope he is home soon. I think it sometimes that to come here was a mistake. I did not think it would be so hard. All the time I was pregnant Doug gave to me teddy bears and the toys. I thought he gave the baby. No. He said. It was time for me to play. He made me laugh just like Roger did before. But no drinking. I think now Doug is drinking again. He doesn't say anything, but I think I know. Don't let the kids hear me cry. One day at a time. Time for bed. Tomorrow is early and a long day at work.

Rachel

Drew is coming by for Sunday dinner. He used to come every day to check up on us, then it was every other week. Now he comes just sometimes. Grandma calls him the "sometimey lizard." She still likes it when he comes, because it's good to have a man in the house—even if he just comes to get a home-cooked meal and to get his feet rubbed. Grandma says this every time Drew visits. And we all laugh. No one really rubs Drew's feet.

Grandma is wearing a good dress with an apron. She wipes her hands on the inside of the apron pockets as she cooks. She has made her spicy beans and a roast with gravy and real potatoes, not the ones that are flakes in a white box that says mashed potatoes. For dessert there's peach cobbler cooling on the stovetop. This is the first day in a long time Grandma's seemed anything like happy. She wants me right up under her, watching how she does the cooking so I can feed my future husband a healthy meal. She shows me how to cut the onions, the carrots, and stir the gravy brown. When she lets me taste the cobbler, she feeds it to me from her hand that still has a salty onion taste.

"Careful now, that's hot."

"I know, Grandma."

I know only a few more things about Grandma than I did when I first came to live with her, because some of things I did know I had to subtract after Aunt Loretta died. Grandma doesn't garden anymore. She doesn't have soft hands. When she comes home from work, the smell of her favorite perfume—still strong—mixed with the day's sweat makes me think of gasoline, like she's a fire ready to burn.

Grandma doesn't watch me close anymore or put the cornstarch-looking powder in my underwear drawer. She talks about getting over or through, like there's nothing much else to do but see whether or not a next day comes. So when Drew comes up the porch today and he gives Grandma flowers that she sets in the middle of the table, there is nothing better. Because Grandma looks something like happy and maybe she'll really rub Drew's feet today—just to have some fun.

Drew seems taller than before. Maybe it's that I'm looking at him now more up and down, when before I would look at him with Aunt Loretta more side to side, making them a picture in my mind. And maybe he looks so big because his hand looks large on the shoulder of his teenaged daughter he's brought with him. Her name is one of the La names that never sound as fancy or flowing as they should. Lakeisha is Drew's fifteen-year-old daughter who lives in North Carolina with her mother and is visiting for the holiday.

"Nice to meet y'all," Lakeisha says grinning and holding in her hand a piece of gum that no one notices but me.

"Go and get Lakeisha one of your sweaters. She gonna get the death of cold in her," Grandma says, tut-tutting as she puts her arms around Lakeisha, who came up to the house without her coat.

"I'm alright, ma'am. Thank you."

"Next time, tell your mama you need to have a coat with you. This ain't no place to be without a winter coat," Grandma says.

Drew introduces me and says he thinks Lakeisha and I will be good friends. "Maybe you could play together."

"I'm too old to play," Lakeisha says like she is throwing something away. She has North Carolina in all the vowels, and still her voice sounds related to Drew's. It's funny how people can sound related.

When we sit down to dinner, Lakeisha asks if she should say the blessing before we eat. She doesn't eat too much of the monkey bread, which Grandma made special for Drew. Lakeisha says sir and ma'am and just like that Grandma wants to know all about her. She asks her questions and fusses over her. She tells Drew that he's got a good girl.

I can tell Lakeisha is none of the things that I think are important. She's not a good student, and she's too loud.

Dinner's done and Drew says he wants to give me something, a present.

"What is it?" I ask.

"Something special."

I like it when people give me clues to how I should respond.

"I don't have a present for you," I say.

"He don't need presents. Open it," Lakeisha says.

I open the package without ripping the wrap. Inside are two books. The smaller one is titled *Black Skin, White Masks* by Frantz Fanon. "That's from me. It may be tough reading now, but hold onto it for a while. Read it when you're ready," he says. "I don't think I got to it until after college, but I wish I had found it sooner. Loretta was reading it—she started reading it . . ." His voice trails off.

The second book is a collection of Hans Christian Andersen's fairy tales.

Drew puts his hand on my shoulder. "This was also with Loretta's things. I'm sure she'd want you to have it."

The red cloth cover has frayed on the bottom right corner. I rub my hands over the spine with its faded gold lettering. On the bottom of the inside cover I see my father's name, Roger Morse, written in crinkly cursive, his handwriting.

I want to cry but don't. I want to fan through the pages of the book. Maybe Pop has left something else here. Maybe there is something here that's more than just his handwriting or his name.

"Grandma, may I be excused?"

"Did I hear a thank you?"

"Thank you, Drew. Thank you very much."

"You're welcome. I'm glad you're happy with it."

"Grandma, may I be excused?"

"You ain't gonna get out of cleaning dishes."

"No, ma'am. I just want to put this away."

"Miss Doris, let the girls go. I'll get these dishes tidied up." Drew stands up as he says this and picks up his plate.

"Ooo-mmm. I never had no mens take care of me." Grandma makes her lizard-eating smile and laughs.

"Grandma? Can I?"

"You can go show Lakeisha your room."

Lakeisha follows me to my room. Before I have closed the door, she's run her hand across everything on my dresser top.

"Ooo, you nasty. Your Grandma let you wear this?" she asks, holding a red lipstick I took from Aunt Loretta's drawer before Grandma boxed up everything else to store or throw away.

Lakeisha talks fast and doesn't let me answer. She has picked up the framed picture of me and Drew and Aunt Loretta in front of the frozen falls.

"Your mom was pretty."

"Aunt Loretta is not my mom."

"Oh?"

"She's my aunt."

"What your mom look like?"

I wish I could say: Just like me, but taller. Like a grown-up me. If I describe what Mor really looks like it will make her seem plain: long blond hair, white skin; she had an accent (and that's important even though it's not something you could tell by looking at her). If I describe her to Lakeisha, it will make Mor seem like any other white person you'd see.

"My mom was light-skinned."

"Light-skinned-ed? For real? That's why you so light?"

"Yeah."

"My mama's not light-skinned-ed but she's pretty. Prettier than her too." She points at the picture of Aunt Loretta.

"How come you don't have a picture of your mama? She done past?"

I nod, holding the book Drew gave me close to my middle like a shield. I wish Lakeisha would go.

"You ever kissed a boy?" she asks.

I shrug my shoulders.

"My brother has a friend I like."

"Oh."

"He's not my real brother. He's cute. But his friend Damon is cuter."

"I have a brother."

"Where he at? He cute?"

"He's not here . . . today."

"He with his daddy, huh?" Lakeisha says with gum in her mouth again. She makes it pop as she chews. "I'ma braid your hair." She grabs the brush from my dresser and starts brushing my hair. "You got good hair. Bet you could grow it real long."

"I guess so." My hair reaches past my shoulders now.

"If I had me some hair like this I'd be workin it." She pretends to swish her hair off her shoulders, then she punches me on the arm.

"You like to dance?"

"I don't know."

"You know how to do the Pac-Man? It's all tired, but it's easy. I could show you."

Lakeisha stands in front of the bed and does the Pac-Man.

She pulls me off the bed. "See, like this," she says, and she does it real slow. "In-out. In-out."

Her feet look like windshield wipers when she does it slow. But then she speeds it up and it looks like dancing.

"You got a radio?"

"Over there."

She walks around to the other side of the bed and turns on the radio. When she turns it on, we both jump because the music plays so loud. Lakeisha turns down the volume quickly and we both laugh.

"You listen to white music."

"That's jazz."

"You ain't got no tapes or nothing?"

I shrug.

She dials through the radio stations. She pauses when one comes in clear.

"Y'all got some sorry radio stations," she says.

She stops turning the dial when she hears "her song." She sings to the chorus. She stands in the mirror and pulls the braids off her face. She makes my brush a microphone. "I'm saving all my love . . . Yes, I'm saving all my love . . ."

When the song is over, she bows and I clap. I wonder how come she seems so brave. There is no part of her she hides. Lakeisha sits with me now on the bed and says, "Wanna hear a story?" I don't have to say yes before she tells me.

Lakeisha tells a story about how this one girl at her school thought she was looking all fly in some white jeans and then she turned around and "you could see she got her menstruations and she didn't know it. We was laughin!"

I hold my book again as a shield wishing I could laugh. Lakeisha might change her mind about me too.

"My dad, he gave me twenty dollars to go to the movies. I'ma buy me some candy and popcorn. You wanna go? You have to have your own money."

"No, thank you," I say.

"No thank you," she says repeating me in a high voice. "Why you talk all proper?"

I shrug.

"My dad said you were really smart. I think you retarded." She pauses. "Not! I'm just playin. Why you so serious?"

I AM HAPPY that Grandma calls us back to the table. We will eat cobbler and then say our good nights, and I will be able to look through each page of this book and find the note Pop must have left for me.

Drew has two helpings of cobbler with ice cream. Grandma has a sweet tooth. She eats two helpings too. She doesn't want a lizard or a rooster anymore. "They gonna have to love all-a this if they want love from me."

I think of how Grandma makes fun of love. And maybe that's the key.

"Miss Doris, you bad. You bad. Careful how those contributions catch up to you," Drew says, pointing to Grandma's "secret" bottle of sherry.

Grandma likes being bad around Drew. She smooths down the front of her dress, the part that stretches across her chest, and she makes a low lizard-eating giggle. Grandma says she feels like a woman when she's being bad. And Lakeisha says, "I'm scared of you, Miss Doris." They all laugh.

Grandma puts the cobbler back in the oven to heat up another helping for Drew. He likes it when the ice cream melts all in it. He talks for a long time about his job at the Salvation Army Harbor Lights Center, the way he wants to landscape his yard with rose bushes and grow a garden with tomatoes and cucumbers and lettuce, and how much he's been missing his sweet Lo. We all hush when he says her name.

Grandma says something first. "It's been too much. Oh, Loretta. I'm missing my baby girl, and Charles . . ."

"You mean Robbie, Grandma."

"I mean Charles and Robbie and that baby too," she says. "I say what I mean."

It's hard to know what Grandma means when she's had the contributions.

And then Drew says thank you and promises to come again soon.

"Rachel, maybe you want to come with us to the parade this weekend? Good spot for watching is up at my job at the Salvation Army on Burnside—not fancy, but you'll be up close."

"Thank you, sir."

"I'ma be there," Lakeisha says.

"Happy to have met you," Grandma says to Lakeisha as they walk to the door. She's made Texas very strong. She turns to Drew. "If you still got her next Sunday, come on to church with us."

"That's a nice invitation. Maybe we will," Drew says. "Lakeisha's a real good singer."

"I heard you all with the radio up," Grandma says, touching Lakeisha's braids. I know she disapproves of braids, but for Lakeisha, today, she makes it okay.

"Lakeisha has a solo in the choir," Drew says.

"You wanna hear it?" Lakeisha asks. She takes the gum out of her mouth, and this time every one sees. Then she takes off her glasses. She is in the middle of the second line of "Amazing Grace" and Grandma joins in.

I hear a voice I have not heard. The choir sang this at Aunt Loretta's funeral. Grandma sings now but she didn't that day. I hear a voice I have not heard. It has the hurt in it.

They finish the song with pitch-perfect harmony. They are holding hands and I want to say that Drew is crying, but I'm not sure. I'm afraid to look. I want to be Lakeisha. She's hugging Grandma, getting the sad stuck feeling out of her with a song. I am fourteen and know that I am black, but I can't make the Gospel sound right from my mouth. I can't help make Grandma's feelings show. They hold hands and Grandma hugs Lakeisha again. I can see what Grandma sees in Lakeisha. It is a reflection.

I smell something burning.

"Good Lord, that last bit of cobbler's burnin," Grandma says and rushes to turn the oven off.

It's late. Drew and Lakeisha have gone home. Beneath my covers I turn on a flashlight and look through the book. There is no note from Pop, but one from Mor on the title page. It says: "Kære Roger, Together, all the stories will have wishes that come true. *Jeg elsker dig.* Nella." And then there's a date from the year I was born. I trace the words with my fingertips. Then I turn to the story I know best: the story of the bird who didn't know he was a swan. Only it reads so different than I remember it. There is an Egyptian, a hunter, and a large comfortable nest the duckling must leave. He didn't decide to go on his own. I wonder: What would Pop remember about this story? What was the wish that came true?

It's late. I close the book. I turn off the flashlight. And every burning thing is off.

Nella

Day 747. Today the woman at the kiosk was staring at us, and she said if the children father was black? Roger never was black. He was charming and fun and handsome. And he loved to have fun. I really felt for him the very first time we met at the base club. We would be at the base club, the airmen club and hang out with friends have a few drinks and dance the night away. He was taken me on picnics around base by Loetz-beuren, the snacks he brought the Saltine crackers, martinis in the thermos and also a blanket so we could smooch. I wasn't ever thinking he was a black. When he said but you cannot be pregnant, we cannot get married, and when I said why not he said cause you are white and I am not. I did not know that was a problem. So many white women were dating NCOs with brown skin, and it was normal to me. I do not think of this thing. I did not say anything to the woman today. She is rude and I did not need give her a answer. Roger said I could not understand because Europa is not the same. He never wanted to come back to America. Is this part of why? The woman was thinking I adopted my children? What does the woman not see? Robbie, the little brown *kys*. He looks like Roger—around the eyes, his nose. His mouth looks like me. Rachel has the same color eyes. They are more pretty for her. Ariel looks just like them when they were babys. More hair. They are my natural children. And look like it.

Rachel

Lakeisha waves to the people below who've come to see the Starlight Holiday Parade. We are on the third floor at the Salvation Army Harbor Lights Center where Drew works. If you sit on the fire escape, like Lakeisha does, it's probably one of the best spots to see the parade. I lean just a little bit out the window instead. Still, I can see the city sign over the Burnside Bridge, which is lit up in daytime during the holidays with the reindeer's nose glowing bright red. The sun's shining after the early morning rain and you can see the snow-covered mountain in the distance to the east. Below, people dressed in their heavy winter coats are seated on lawn chairs that line the street. The marching bands, the cheerleading squads, the floats, and the fancy decorated cars go by.

There isn't a queen for this parade, but that's what Lakeisha looks like she's practicing to be, waving to the crowd below.

Lakeisha could never be queen. Her glasses fog up. And she flicks her wrist too fast for the wave. She waves anyway.

"My brother's friend. He's as tall as that guy. That one playing the trumpet," Lakeisha says pointing to the band crossing down Burnside.

"Where?"

"Right there," she says and points. "If you weren't so scary you could see him good from out here."

"I'm not scared."

"You ain't coming out here."

"So. It's cold. I'm cold."

Lakeisha has fog in her glasses and her breath comes out in a cloud. "Okay, scaredy cat, come on let's get something to eat. This is tired anyway. Watching a parade from a bum house ain't no fun."

Lakeisha crawls back through the window from the fire escape. She uses my shoulder for balance and jumps to the floor almost knocking me down. "Come on, dang."

"So you're hungry," Drew says. "Well, you're just in time for lunch."

"I don't want to eat with no bums," Lakeisha says.

"Lakeisha, you show some respect. These are men. They're trying to make a change."

"I think it smells good," I say.

"It should. We've got a special holiday meal."

"How come I can't have McDonald's?" Lakeisha asks. Drew gives her a harsh look and says, "Why don't you follow Rachel's lead? Show some manners."

Lakeisha and I get in line along with the others. Not all of the men live at the center. Some still live on the street and they smell like it. Lakeisha holds her nose when she grabs a tray.

We sit down as close to the door as possible at a table where there are only two men on the far end. Lakeisha has put only peas and potatoes on her plate. "That food looks like dookie," she says. "I'm not eating bum food."

"Whatever," I say, eating the turkey I've topped with lots of gravy. It doesn't taste so bad to me.

As the cafeteria fills up, so does our table, and someone sits down next to me.

"Good afternoon," the man says.

We both look up and nod then look away. The man looks like an old cowboy on TV. His skin's real wrinkled, real tan. He's got sideburns and long hair pulled back in a ponytail. Even though he's missing three front teeth, his smile looks like it's ready to bite.

"Lookie there, at those eyes," the man says and pats my shoulder. "You're gonna be a real heartbreaker."

Lakeisha looks up from her plate. She laughs.

"Excuse me," I say and get up and carry away my tray.

Lakeisha's right behind me. "Who don't have manners now? Why you got be so conceited? You don't want a boy-friend who's a bum?"

"LAKEISHA'S COMING OVER," Grandma says the next day. "Y'all is gonna watch each other. And none of that trouble."

"Why?"

"I'm gonna go with Drew."

It's Aunt Loretta's birthday. They're going to the cemetery.

"Can I go?"

"No. Now hush up."

"I just said I want to go."

"Hush. No need to be thinking things. Go in and straighten up your room. You're gonna have company."

Lakeisha and I eat Grandma's homemade cookies and the Dorito chips Lakeisha brought. We eat it watching three episodes of *The Brady Bunch* in a row.

"Y'all ain't got cable?"

"Nope."

"That's how come you can't dance. I be watching MTV. Me and my friend know most of the 'Thriller' dance just from watching. You wanna learn it?"

"No."

"How come you so boring?"

"I'm not."

"You know what? One time I found my mama's birth control. And a fake penis. Bet you got something like that somewhere here. I'll show you."

Lakeisha goes into the bathroom first, and then into Grandma's room where I am not allowed to go. We look through the drawers and hall closets and then go down to the basement.

"What's this?"

Downstairs are boxes and boxes of Goodwill finds, of old clothes, of Aunt Loretta's things, and then I see a box that I don't recognize with my name on it. It's not Grandma's handwriting or Aunt Loretta's either.

When I open the box I see it's all wrong. This isn't me—not from a me I can recognize. Then I realize these are things from that day—a few books, my only pair of dress shoes, sweaters, two pairs of pants, three stuffed animals, and the sheets that were on my bed. And the pajamas that I had folded and tucked under my pillow.

And there's a newspaper page folded in half, page B3: "Police say they are continuing their investigation to rule out foul play. Witnesses indicate possible suspects . . . 'The only person who may really know,' said Capt. Ronald Veliveau of the Chicago police, 'is that brave kid who's fighting to survive now. She might not remember. She might not want to.' "

"What you reading?"

I hold the newspaper trying to make my hands still. They won't stop shaking.

"Come on," I say, putting the paper in my pocket, "let's go watch TV."

When Grandma gets home she is "all through" early. It's not even eight o'clock when she goes to bed. A full bottle of contribution is empty again.

I want to ask her what she knows about that day, but she's deep into sleeping—so much that she's started to snore.

UP ON THE ROOF *Mor told us things she remembered about her childhood self: how she saved the wishbone in her jewelry box until she really needed a wish to come true; how she always ate her dinner one food at a time. She told us about all the things that mattered to her, about everything that counted and how it all added up to a childhood she had never remembered being so good before.*

"Math was my favorite subject in school," she said in Danish. She said she could find herself better in numbers. She liked the way there was always only a single answer.

On that last day Mor took us up to the roof, she had calculated the difference between what we couldn't have and her ability to watch us want. The difference between her pain and ours, she decided, measured nine stories high.

I HAVE NEVER told anyone and maybe I should have. That day there was a man. And if only I had told, then Mor wouldn't be all to blame.

Nella

Day 751. I am stupid. He was drinking with his friend when he knows alcohol is not allowed in the house. Like Roger he wants to be fun. Having fun all the time. He says this isn't fun. It is not fun. Waking up in the middle of the night to the baby. Three hours sleeping. Going to work. Seeing Rachel and Robbie sad. Children should play outside in the summer but here is not safe. They do not know the place. They say they are bored. I take them to the park Saturday and Sunday. I have taken home from the library books for the kids to read. Doug says he will not be in the house drinking again. He says he will stop. Was it a mistake coming here? There was no where else to go. I couldn't go home. Doug said he would help. Now he goes out all night sometimes. Not coming home. Oh, no, the babys crying.

Brick

Brick was transfixed by the scar above Laronne's son's left eye. Maybe he was cut by pirates, but then he was saved. Maybe he fought some scary monster who scraped him with a giant claw. He knew the scar was the result of neither of these things or anything like it—but to have a scar so big and survive seemed incredible to Brick. Laronne's son, Greg, must have done something heroic, he thought. Even if it was just not being too scared.

Brick was no hero. He was too scared to go back to the hospital; too scared to play outside if the pigeon man found him; too scared even to go back home since the night the policemen came by.

He hid beneath his bed when he realized they had come for him and not for one of his mother's new friends. *What did he know about the accident,* they asked. His mother was in a deep haze when she opened the door. When she said her boy wasn't home—even though it was dark and after nine p.m.—she really thought he wasn't.

Brick had spent every night since then at Laronne's. His mom didn't seem to mind. Laronne sent him to school with a lunch packed the same as her boy's. And they walked to the city bus together every day.

Greg was good at playing big brother. He was, one, bigger than Brick. Two, he had lots of jokes, knock-knocks and booger jokes that he liked to share with Brick. Three, he was quick with his hands, so quick with the tap-on-the-shoulder trick he'd get Brick every time. And four, he knew dozens of ghost stories and monster stories that he told Brick each night in a whisper in the dark of the room that they shared.

Brick took Greg's ribbing in stride. In fact, he liked it. Not the monster stories so much, but he had scarier things in his dreams already.

"That guy in Atlanta snatched up another kid yesterday," Greg said.

"Enough of that talk at the dinner table," Laronne's husband, David, said.

Brick made a note to himself: Be careful of the pigeon man and of the child snatcher.

Laronne's son snatched at Brick with a monster sound. "Arrghhhh."

Brick jumped and coughed as milk caught in his throat.

"I said that's enough," David yelled. "You're not gonna stop until your roughhousing chokes the boy to death. And no more talk of that evilness. He's not just a child snatcher. He's a child killer."

"Yes, sir."

Dinner continued in silence until there was a knock at the door.

Laronne went to answer it. When Brick heard Laronne call the visitor "sir" and then "officer," he fled the table.

"My stomach hurts," he said and ran to the bathroom. He could hear the police officer introduce himself. "We understood you might be able to help with the investigation of Nella Fløe and her children. I want to go over some information with you."

"Have you found the boyfriend yet? He's been missing since it happened."

"We're checking into it. We haven't found him."

"You know," Laronne said. "Brick is the one you should be talking to. He lives a couple of floors below Nella and the kids. He said he saw a man up there that day. Brick?" Laronne shouted. "Brick?" she called again. "He's here—he's visiting."

"That the boy said something in the newspaper?"

"That's him," she said. "Sweet boy."

"Can't imagine what it's doing to him to have seen that," the officer said. "It took a bit to find him cause of the different name. We went to talk to him a few days ago. His mama said he wasn't home, but sure didn't seem like she could figure out what was up or down the way she looked."

Laronne knocked on the bathroom door. "Brick, you okay?"

Brick opened the door slowly. "Yes?"

"Baby can you come tell the police officer what you saw?"

Laronne had not asked him about the accident since the day in the stairwell. He considered it their secret, a special bond—what he knew, what he didn't tell.

"You can tell him," she said. "You don't have to be afraid of that man." Brick was thinking of the pigeon man and how easy it would be for the pigeon man to find him. He was thinking of what the pigeon man told him to say. He was thinking of Roger's confession: But he couldn't imagine Roger's hands like that—pushing a boy, a woman, or a girl—just to see how they'd fly. But he had said: "*Maybe I did it.*" Thinking of all these things, he wasn't sure who to blame.

"You saw a man on the roof? How tall was he, son? Was he black? White? What?" the policeman asked.

Brick shrugged.

"Well, how is he going to know that—when the man wasn't but a speck standing so high up?" David said watching Brick.

"Sir, these are standard questions. We're trying to get an idea of who we're looking for. Son, do you know?"

"Yes," Brick said and then tried to describe a man he'd never seen. "About six feet tall . . . orange hair." He stopped. But that was someone he did see, he thought. That was the man at the bottom of the stairs the day after the accident. It was funny how imagination worked. He could make up the description of a man only by thinking of men he'd seen. "I mean maybe it was an orange hat. A ski cap. And a blue shirt. He looked like maybe he was mean," Brick said. The officer wrote down every word he said. It was easy this imagining thing.

"What else can you remember? Any other details?"

Brick thought of what else he could say. "Big ring on his finger. Tall. White?"

"Sounds like a punk we talked to last week," the officer said.

"The pigeon man?" Brick asked.

"He the guy you saw?"

"Doug," Laronne interrupted. "He must mean the boyfriend. He had red hair," Laronne says.

"Anything else son?"

"No sir."

"Is that all? Can you tell us what happens next?" Laronne asked as the officer put his notebook away.

"Look, ma'am," he said, "We don't have much to go on here. And nobody wants to be right about this any way you cut it."

"But we have to still try to find out," Laronne said. "Don't we have to find out why?"

THE NEXT MORNING when Brick saw the school bus coming, he said to Laronne's boy, "I forgot my homework. I gotta go back."

As the bus sped away, Brick ran. He ran the ten blocks to his building's courtyard and looked up toward the window that was his own.

He was certain he saw his mother's hand drag the curtain closed. He kept looking up at that closed window until he heard the voices of boys behind him, running to catch the bus like he should have been. He had been looking up all this time. Nothing fell from this sky.

Laronne

When Laronne went to the hospital again, she saw a heavy-set black woman rocking in the chair next to the girl's bed.

"Excuse me, ma'am," Laronne said touching the woman's shoulder.

The woman looked up at her blankly.

"I packed up the apartment," Laronne said. "I'd be happy to send the boxes to you if you want."

The woman stared at her.

"Those boxes have Rachel's things," Laronne said, pointing at the two boxes she had brought a few days earlier. "I thought she might . . . well." Laronne paused. "The rest of the things—they're boxed up and ready to go. I hope that's okay. I wanted to help. I was her mother's boss."

"Her mother . . . That don't describe what that woman was. Nothing describes her. I don't want nothing of that woman's. You keep it. You can throw it out."

The woman went back to rocking and stroked the girl's hair. "You gonna be alright. Doris is gonna make it all right now."

Brick

At the bus station two nights later, with the money he found and the money he stole from his mother's coat, purse, and coin jar, Brick had enough to buy his ticket out of town.

"Kansas City, huh?" said the bus driver as he took his ticket.

"Yes, sir." It was as far as his money could get him.

He had looked at the map in the school library like Roger would, seeing targets and enemy territory. At first he'd picked the largest dot on the map that he could find farthest away from Chicago—Los Angeles.

But then Laronne told him that the fuzzy-haired girl with the blue blue eyes was going to a hospital in Portland, Oregon, soon. Did he know where that was?

Brick sat in a seat close to the front. He had packed a tooth-brush, a T-shirt, and Roger's harmonica. He'd saved the cook-ies and apples from his free lunch the last couple of days and bought the biggest bag of sunflower seeds in the corner gro-cery store.

Sitting there on the bus, Brick felt heroic. Wouldn't the girl with the fuzzy hair and the blue blue eyes be surprised when she saw him? It would go like this: Hi, my name's Brick. I used to live downstairs. I met your dad, and he said tell you this. And Brick would launch into the story that Roger told him and then play her the song. Hum. Mmmm. Hum.

To-Kansas-City was a long bus ride, and Brick was happy to get off. For the next week he hunted for lost coins and empty soda bottles to find a way to buy the ticket the rest of the way. He hid the first couple of nights behind the stairs at the Y and then in an old boxing gym near the bus station. He had learned the art of invisibility. Stay quiet. Nod yes. Speak only when spoken to.

He wasn't used to this city's sounds. The drunks—who in the day were students or bankers or clerks in the stores—came home when the streets were empty and slammed the bike stor-age door loud enough to wake him most nights. Sometimes he'd wake to the sounds of the small scenes that spilled out onto the street in front of the massage parlor when one of the regular old men didn't get his regular girl, or the sounds of barking dogs when the young men finally exited the bar down the street.

The sounds from the street alarmed him less than those of his dreams. He was happy when he could wake up before screaming. This night he didn't. His scream attracted the attention of a young woman and man—who had taken refuge in the gym too.

"Damn kid, you nearly made me pee myself," the man said.

"You thought it was a monster! Ha ha," the young woman laughed mocking him. "He's a kid. He's just a kid."

"What you doing here, kid? Go away."

Brick was paralyzed.

"If you got something to pay us with, you can stay."

"What?" Brick asked.

"Rent. This is our spot. You can stay if you got some rent money."

Brick figured he was only a day or so away from having enough coins to buy another bus ticket. He'd exchanged the money he'd collected for bills and stuffed it into his sock—a trick he once saw one of his mother's friends do with a knife. Please, please, he thought. He couldn't spend any more time looking for a place to sleep. And he didn't have money to spare.

"Leave him alone," the woman said. Brick could see she came from money. She had straight teeth, and around her neck she wore a gold chain with a pearl. But she was dressed the same as other runaways he'd seen hanging out by the bus station and downtown. Her youth looked rubbed down—smudged like her black eyeliner. He knew they were junkies and meant no harm. Like his mother, they just needed their fix to go on.

"I don't have any money," Brick said.

When the young man started toward him, Brick cowered instead of running. He made himself a heavy weight, but not heavy enough for the young man not to lift him upside down and shake him the way the older neighborhood kids did for sport and for change. Everything in Brick's pockets—a marble, the newspaper story, and his harmonica—fell to the ground. The stash in his sock didn't shake free. The man set him down.

Brick hiked his jeans up. He straightened his sweat jacket on his small shoulders. "That's all you got?" the man said examining the marble, the newspaper clipping, and the harmonica.

Brick nodded.

Turning to the girl, holding the harmonica high, the man said, "What you think we could get for this?"

"You can't get shit for that. But if we had a monkey could play it, we'd be rich and high and happy." She laughed at her own joke.

"Hey, monkey." Brick knew the young man meant him. "You play."

Was it a question or an order?

The young man hit Brick on the head hard enough for Brick to stumble.

"Play." It was no question. The young man handed Brick the harmonica.

Brick played the tune that Roger taught him, slowly. He played the soul of who he was. It was as if the harmonica could sound without his breath. It breathed without lungs.

"Nice job, monkey. I'm gonna let you stay here tonight, and tomorrow you go with us up to by the highway. Bet you'll score us something good."

"He's so cute." The young woman chuckled each time she spoke.

"You see it?" the young man said turning to her. "It puts on a sad monkey face and plays that thing. Girl, we're gonna be set. People gotta help us if we have a kid." They kissed then, a long nasty kiss that made the young woman press herself against the young man.

Brick wasn't a monkey or an it, but he felt like one until the woman looked directly at him that moment and said, "It looks scared. Are you scared?"

"Yes, ma'am."

"Don't call me ma'am. I'm nineteen. My name's Lisa."

"He doesn't need to know names. He needs to keep his monkey ass in check."

"Come here, monkey," the woman named Lisa said.

Brick took steps so small toward her the distance was like a tightrope walk.

"You like to cuddle don't you, monkey? Come on here by me."

Her arm was around him and she nestled his face onto her chest, pressing him against her partially bare breast.

"That's my tittie, monkey. Don't get ideas," the man said.

"He's scared," Lisa said. "He won't be able to play if he's scared."

"Give him this." The young man handed Lisa a small white pill. "That'll keep him rested."

Brick took the pill from Lisa. Swallowed. After a few minutes he got a soft melting feeling, then a melted feeling.

"You look like you could use some love," Lisa said. She pet his head and caressed his shoulder. "You go to sleep little monkey. We got a big day ahead."

Rachel

Grandma's garden's dying and the mad look on her face stays there all the time.

At night Grandma sits in her rocking chair on the porch where she can see the men who lean into passing cars. Everyone knows they're selling drugs, but the police don't stop them. I tell Grandma it's dangerous to be out there at night, but she won't listen.

When Grandma sits out there, she talks at the top of her voice to nobody in particular about pride. About the way black folks used to care about more than loud thumping music and gold chains. She's only so bold when she's drinking the sherry Miss Verle brings.

IN HIGH SCHOOL I still don't have a best friend, even though I know how to answer the questions differently now.

I'm black. I'm from northeast Portland. My grandfather's eyes are this color. I've lived here mostly my whole life. I'm black. I'm black, I know.

I spend a lot of time reading at the library that's next to the high school. There's a new black literature section. It's four whole shelves. I found one book of poetry about a girl who has a white father and a black mother. I have never read anything like that before. And I'm reading the book that Drew gave me, *Black Skin, White Masks*. But I'm not so sure I agree with what it says. There is a chapter called "The Man of Color and the White Woman." Just that title makes me mad. I can't explain why. The book uses the word *Negro* like they did in the old days. Jesse Jackson wants us to be African-American now. I don't know if this is a good idea. I don't know any black people who have even been to Africa. It's like calling me Danish-American even though I've never been to Denmark. But at least I speak Danish. I don't know a single black person who speaks Swahili or any of those other African things they speak. Then there's page 173: "Wherever he goes, the Negro remains a Negro." That makes me think of how the other black girls in school think I want to be white. They call me an Oreo. I don't want to be white. Sometimes I want to go back to being what I was. I want to be nothing.

Grandma keeps saying what I need to study is typing. That way I can work in a nice office one day. "A pretty girl's gonna go somewhere. Now that's a fact. Long as she keeps that pretty to herself and then her husband." Miss Verle agrees with Grandma. She says a pretty girl can take aim at whatever she wants and have it—even something like a good office job. Grandma and Miss Verle think secretary when they say this; they think of it as something good. Grandma thinks she's dreaming big when she says I can have a three-bedroom house on Albina or Killingsworth or maybe near Irving Park (she calls it Irvington), and a husband, and a Toyota that has the new-car smell. She wants me to be able to buy whatever I want at the Fred Meyer without paying attention to what vegetable is on sale and without worrying about bringing double coupons. She thinks a shopping spree at Meier & Frank for a Sunday hat and a new church dress every few months is living in style.

Grandma sees these things when she talks about them and gestures with her hands like she's painting brush strokes in the air. The way Grandma paints her dream for me, there's a low sky.

Grandma's dreams come from hearing about Up North when she was growing up in Texas on a farm, on a road that had no name. Grandma's dream is bigger than her life. I guess at Mor's dreams: having a husband, a family, love. That's the way I would list them. But then I think about it again—her dream maybe was feeling the way she felt with Doug, the way she would smile easy, she would laugh easy, she would play. At least at first. Then the sky in her dream got low too.

Sometimes I think Grandma and Mor are two sides of the same coin. They are two sides of a coin that I can hold in my hand at the same time.

I KNOW I am not interesting to Grandma anymore—what with my new ways. My new ways are back talk. I call it explaining. My new ways are wearing my shirts too tight. I call it fashion. My new ways are paying too much attention to boys. I call it being lonely.

There's a new boy at our high school named John Bailey. He's a basketball player. He's very tall and very handsome and the same color brown as Pop. John Bailey knows that I am black. The first thing John Bailey said to me was "You must be the prettiest girl in the Jack & Jill here."

I guess you could say he's my boyfriend now. He likes the shirts I wear.

The first time I kissed John Bailey it was in the back hallway by the gym. The second time I kissed John Bailey it was in his basement room laying down.

Kissing John Bailey felt real good. It was like everything that's the outside me—the me that people see—made all of what is really me feel really good. When John Bailey touches me, I know this is the skin I want to be in. Sometimes, when his mom works nights and he doesn't have basketball practice, I go to his house after school.

When I come home late, I tell Grandma I was at the library.

"Fast girls go to the library too," she says, and it is like she is looking right into the center of me.

"Okay, Grandma." I'm caught. How does she know?

"Don't do what your mama did. Some people ain't figured to take care of babies. Specially some people, like your mama—hoing herself to that no-count man."

Grandma never mentions my mother.

"It ain't respectable. Don't be like your mama—sniffin around life like the only nose you've got is the one between your legs."

So this is the part of me that is Mor? It is the part of me that wants to be touched. It is the part that makes me want someone to touch me.

"You didn't know the good parts of my mother," I say, and I hope that I won't cry.

"A woman made of parts is a dangerous thing," Grandma says. "You never know when she'll throw away a piece you may need. Your mama was a crazy lady."

And then I yell at Grandma, like I've never yelled at her, or at anyone before. I say, "You're a damn lie—that newspaper story proves it. My mom didn't do a damn thing!"

MOR WALKED US *up three flights of stairs to the roof. She carried Ariel in her arms. Robbie and I, we followed two steps behind. Mor had taken us up to the roof three times that week—each time closer to the edge.*

On the evenings on the rooftop, Mor wrapped her arms, like wings, around our shoulders and breathed onto our necks to keep us warm. Robbie and I fought about who got to crawl on her lap.

Mor hadn't seemed right that last week since the fight with Doug. Robbie had gone without his pills for two days; Ariel's diaper was often wet. Mor's blue eyes had faded into a fuzzy stare. Her long blond hair fell in limp strands. And when she spoke, I could see the space for the tooth she lost in the fight with her boyfriend. I didn't want to be like her anymore; I didn't want her smooth white skin.

"YOU WEREN'T THERE. You don't know what happened," I say. "Up on the roof, there was a man."

Laronne

From the rooftop Laronne could see the puddle where the shrine had been. The swing set—repaired to draw attention from what should be a grave—shone too new. Tattered yellow police tape clung stubbornly to a bench leg.

To come up here, to the rooftop, Nella must have imagined she was going to a place like any other place on a map, Laronne thought.

To climb the flight of stairs with a baby in her arms and her two children in tow. One flight, then two. Nella must have thought she was going somewhere.

Laronne had spent many nights reading through Nella's diaries. She could almost hear Nella's soft voice in her ear as she read.

In the last two journals—the ones she had written since she

came to the U.S.—Nella's voice sounded more like a plea. One entry that was undated, Laronne knew, must have been from two weeks ago: "Never have I been thinking of my children as black. How to learn all these things that might hurt them? I want to pull out my tongue if I made them sad . . . It makes me so sad I said those things to them. I want them to know how much I love them. I love them and will keep them safe." The words haunted Laronne.

Two weeks before the accident, Laronne had complimented Nella on her new scarf.

"Why thank you," Nella responded with a fake British accent copying Laronne's own silly talk: "I'm going to have tea with the queen," Laronne would say like a true Brit when complimented.

"Now did your special fellow give that to you?" That day Laronne's voice was high like she was talking to her two cats. It was a note away from a tickle.

"Nope." Nella had laughed as if she had been tickled. "It's from my little jigaboos." She said it with all love.

"Your?" Laronne paused.

"My little jigaboos. That's what Doug calls them. It's so cute."

"Nella. Don't say that again. It's not cute."

The first time Laronne heard the word—the first time it was directed at her—she wasn't even ten years old. *Nigger, jigaboo*—they were the same. The words came so fast she barely understood that it was language. She was waiting for the bus after the city spelling bee finals. Out in the second round because she spelled *fugitive* with an *a,* it was time to go home. Still she felt good and full of herself. She was wearing her older cousin's hand-me-down pants (a little on the short side)—but they were store-bought not handmade, a fuzzy sweater she thought she would keep forever, and a warm blue winter coat—double-breasted. Next time, she thought, I'll study more words.

Who knows why children decide to bully another. It started with kicking up dirt on Laronne. The white boys not much bigger—not much older—waited at the same bus stop with her in the good part of town. Kicking up dirt, you know the way they do. Like it was just an accident. "Oops sorry." And then they would laugh.

Laronne had been taught to ignore bullies. But as the boys got louder, they kicked the dirt and laughed and laughed harder, and they said, "Oops, sorry, highwater girl." "Oops, sorry, ugly face." "Sorry, straw head." "Sorry, jigaboo." "Sorry, nigger." And then it was *nigger, nigger, nigger* sung and shouted like a Top 40 pop song. *Nigger, nigger, nigger, jigaboo.*

Laronne's mother had her own story of "The First Time I Was Called a Nigger." Her father did too. These stories were passed down to Laronne when it happened to her that day. They did not help her stop crying. They did not soothe.

"Nigger. Nella, it means nigger."

"Oh goodness. Oh my goodness," Nella had said. "Oh goodness, no—I didn't know. Oh, I knew about the other word . . ."

"Nigger?" Laronne said it again as if she were preempting Nella from saying it.

"Oh, that's a terrible word. I . . ."

"It's the same thing." Laronne's voice had more anger in it than she meant.

"I didn't know," Nella had said again, in almost a whisper. "Do you think, Laronne—Laronne do you think the kids know? Is it something you would just know . . . the word?"

Laronne didn't know how to answer. "Nella, they know you love them."

"But I don't ever want them to think—to think I'd let anything hurt them."

"They know."

"I want them to really know."

And like a flash, a second thought, Nella had said: "I don't think Doug meant—means that." But the way Nella had said it, Laronne thought she didn't seem so sure. Whatever authority that was in Nella's voice came from a desire to believe—not belief—that the man she left her marriage for wasn't the worst thing she could have wished on her kids.

THESE WHITE GIRLS *think all they need is love.*
What might Nella have seen that day? Not tall buildings, or city streets, not the treeless courtyard below. Try hard as she might, Laronne couldn't sweep away the view. But Nella must have.

What must Nella have seen? Not the ground, but an expanse. It was this step and then another, then another. This was what Nella saw. This was what Nella did. She was journeying to where her love was enough, and it could fill the sky.

Nella

Day 759. I wanted a drink today. But I didn't. What did I do? Laronne told me today about the word Doug says—I do not want to write it down. I did not know. I don't think they know what it means. Never have I been thinking of my children as black. How to learn all these things that might hurt them? I want to pull out my tongue if I made them sad. I don't think Doug understands the meaning. I don't. I don't. I don't know how to ask him. He is coming home soon. He says he is not drinking. I am not sure. When I come home from work, he sleeps on the couch. Then he goes hanging out with his friends. It makes me so sad I said those things to them. I want them to know how much I love them. I love them and will keep them safe. My children are one half of black. They are also one half of me. I want them to be anything. They are not just a color that people see.

Rachel

"If it ain't one thing, it's another."

That's Grandma's way of cursing when she sees the porch window's broken.

"Lord have mercy if our people ain't just gonna do ourselves in."

We don't know for sure, but it's Drew's best guess that one of the kids who hangs out on the corner threw a rock to scare us. They're tired of Grandma's loud talk from the porch. It makes Grandma mad, but also sad that the neighborhood has changed so much.

"Them closing the drive-through dairy was one thing," Grandma says. "But not feeling safe in your own home . . . It was the best of the best black folk living around here when I first come. And the rest of them hard workers, mostly from the shipyards—not like them kids ruinin things just to get some new sneakers. Look at us now."

Even I can see it. Things just aren't the same. Across the street Mrs. Lewis put bars on her windows, and the neighbor next door got a big dog. There have been three break-ins on this street in the last month. On the block where there was a real grocery store, now there's just a convenience store, a liquor store, a church, and a place that you can buy hair. The closest grocery store is a twenty-minute bus ride away. And someone spray-painted graffiti on the Alberta Street community center mural of the Reverend Martin Luther King. My ex-friend Tracy used to say I lived in the ghetto, which made me think of the TV show *Good Times*. A ghetto has tall buildings and empty lots, trash all over the street and city noise. Here the houses are two stories; the houses have trees in front and everyone has a yard. I always told Tracy she was wrong, but now I think Tracy was right. The ghetto looks different in different places, but if you live there, it makes you feel the same.

"Miss Doris, don't you worry," Drew says. "I'll take care of it."

"Now how am I gonna leave this child alone knowing those hooligans tryin to get me?"

Grandma's bags have been packed for two days. She's going on the train to Seattle for the church convention.

"How about if I stay on, Miss Doris?" Drew says. He offers to sleep on the couch and see to it that I'm fed and safe at night while she's gone. At first Grandma says she can't let Drew do that.

"Go on. Things'll be fine. Now let me call somebody see if I can get this here patched up."

Grandma looks at me real stern and says, "Now don't be giving Drew no trouble."

"Yes, ma'am."

IT'S STRANGE TO have Drew stay over. I'm in bed with the door a little bit open. I can hear the television show he's watching. If I scoot to the top of the bed, I can see the top of his head through the open sliver of the door.

It makes me think: No man has slept in this house since the day Pop left to go to the air force. And that's been a long time now.

I settle down into the blankets and close my eyes. I'll be safe tonight. I won't be alone.

I think I would like it if Drew lived here full-time because he makes French toast for breakfast. I have two slices and he has four. He doesn't ask me why I hold the fork and knife in opposite hands while I eat. (It's the Danish way.) And when I say, "*Tak for mad*" —which is what you say after a meal—he says, "Well, alright," and smiles. When he's done eating, he makes a fake burp and pats his pushed-out stomach, making it round. He's not all about formality like Grandma.

Drew reads not just one, but three newspapers during breakfast: the *Oregonian* and the *New York Times* and the *Wall Street Journal*. He starts with the front page, then reads almost every page to the end like he's reading a book. He doesn't read the comics like Grandma does. Drew isn't interested in the funnies. He wants to know about what's happening in the world. He has all kinds of things to say about our times, like how racial injustice is worse than when he was growing up, how apartheid has to end real soon and Nelson Mandela must be free, how the government doesn't care about these new drugs like crack taking over our neighborhoods; how ketchup can't be a vegetable to anybody; and how he never thought he'd live to see the day that the young brothers would be killing each other over tennis shoes.

He goes on and on. "And what does it matter?" he says today. He's reading a story about a protest that happened downtown yesterday. About a month ago, an Ethiopian man was killed over in Southeast by a bunch of skinheads, wearing swastikas. They chased the man down and beat him to death with a bat.

"Even if the Ethiopian kid threw the first punch, it's no reason to beat the boy to death with a bat," Drew says as if he's talking to me, but really he's talking to himself out loud. "Mark my words: Lines are being drawn."

I nod my head. He talks about the news this way, like he's in a conversation with the world, but it's really just himself. I pay attention. I know he wants me to listen in.

FOR THE MOST part, the weekend goes on like it normally does. I go to the library. I watch some TV. It's normal but also special that Drew's here.

Tonight Drew's going out and I have to "hold down the fort" by myself for a couple of hours. He's running the shower so long it would make Grandma tap her remote control on her bedroom wall. You can tell how steamy Drew's shower water is by the drips of dew that are collecting on the bottom of the doorframe. Not that I'm looking or anything, but also there's a powerful soap scent coming from the room. It smells like the woods only clean. Drew smells as good as a homemade loaf of bread.

He gets dressed in all black for a concert by a singer I've never heard of. "Etta James? You've never heard of Etta James?"

"No, sir."

"You ever heard the blues?"

"Kind of." And I think if he means like some old black guys on a porch with guitars then I have seen that on TV.

"Kind of?" he asks, and he gets into the low part of his voice like Deacon James. "The blues ain't something you could kind of know."

"Well, is it like jazz? My mom used to listen to jazz."

"Young lady, we've got to get you schooled. You're going with me tonight."

"Sir, I can't go. It's a bar."

"It's a restaurant too. And I'm not doing any drinking," Drew says. "It'll be fine. We just won't mention it to Miss Doris. Come on. Go get dressed."

A special date with Drew calls for a special outfit—not church clothes but as close to grown-up woman clothes as I can get. So I wear a black sweater that used to be Aunt Loretta's, a black skirt, high heels, and a purple brooch that Grandma found beneath her seat on the bus one day.

THE RESTAURANT IS smoky and dark. Everyone seems to know Drew's name. We sit close to the stage.

"This okay?" Drew asks.

Of course, everything's okay. I smile.

We sit for a few moments listening to the band warm up. "Rachel, you're sure these are good seats? I can't hear myself think."

"Maybe because I can only hear half of everything," I shout back at him, pointing to my deaf left ear.

Drew squints his eyes and cocks his head to the side. He's a big question mark. And I wonder what he really knows. I know when people ask how it was I came to live with her, Grandma says, "Her mama couldn't do right by her." And no one ever asks where Pop has gone.

I'm not going to explain to Drew what I mean because I like thinking of myself this way: like nothing is wrong with me at all. I wave my hands to say "never mind" and turn to look at the stage again.

That's when the waitress with red-orange lipstick and braids piled on top of her head comes over. She leans over Drew a little too close, I think, and kisses him closer to his mouth than his cheek.

"Who you got with you?"

"This is Lo's niece."

"Well, bless your heart."

"I'm looking out for Rachel for the weekend while her grandmother is gone."

"Lord have mercy and takin her to a place like this is what you call lookin out?" I look around when she says this. This is a restaurant, just like Drew says, but more of a bar or a lounge. There is no one here even near my age.

"She'll be fine. She's incorruptible. She's got a good head on her shoulders too."

"So what can I get you, sweetie?" the waitress asks.

ETTA JAMES IS stuffed together like Grandma—a big, squishy capsule—and she's light-skinned like me. She's got the gravel to her voice when she sings the loud parts (and the parts that are kind of nasty too). She also has that soft spot in her voice when she sings songs that are about being lonely and sad.

The last song, which is an encore, is a long, slow song. I clap and clap. And stand and clap. I want to say this the way Grandma would if she agreed: I like me some Etta James! It feels like it's the only way to say it to make the meaning good.

Drew laughs.

"I wish Lakeisha could appreciate the things you do. I know it's been hard on her, me not being around. But that girl's got no interest in nothing but trouble. Grant me the serenity to accept the things I cannot change. It's all I can do. I try to be there for her: phone calls, letters. Those are just words. And she's so grown. Just not grown up. Lord, help her."

It's like I'm not there as Drew says this, because I can tell that he's sad and I don't know what to say to make him feel better. Me, personally, I think Lakeisha's not too smart. Because if I had a dad like Drew I'd make sure he was proud of me. I'd make sure he knew that I liked having him around.

When we get home to Grandma's house, everything I notice is what is different about Drew being here. His blanket's bunched up on the couch, and his bag is halfway hidden beneath the coffee table. And the other thing I notice is not something you can see, but a feeling. It's that feeling Mor called *hyggeligt*. It means something like comfort and home and love all rolled into one. That feeling went away when Aunt Loretta died, but somehow, it's here tonight.

AFTER I BRUSH my teeth, I go to the living room to say thank you and good night.

"You're welcome," Drew says. "Sleep tight."

"So, I guess I know what the blues is now," I say smiling.

"Oh, yeah?" There's a smirk on Drew's face, not like he wants to laugh at what I'm going to say, but he's going to pay attention real close. "What do you know?"

"Well, I would explain the blues this way: Like for me, I imagine inside of a person there's a blue bottle, you know?"

I feel shaky when I say this but also good. I've never told anyone about the blue bottle before.

"Yeah?"

"The bottle is where everything sad or mean or confusing can go. And the blues—it's like that bottle. But in the bottle there's a seed that you let grow. Even in the bottle it can grow big and green. It's full of all those feelings that are in there, but beautiful and growing too."

"Yes, Rachel," Drew says, "that makes a lot of sense to me."

In bed later, I stare at the ceiling for a long time. I am thinking: What if Mor knew about the blues? What if she had thought that sometimes there's a way to take the sadness and turn it into a beautiful song?

GRANDMA TAKES AN extra day away because the trains aren't running on time.

That's okay by me. It gives me an extra day to plan a welcome-home dinner and a celebration of three straight-A report cards in a row. Drew doesn't mind staying the extra night watching me either. This way the window will be fixed by the time Grandma gets back, and she won't have to worry about a thing.

"Welcome home, Grandma." I yell when she opens the door and steps inside with Miss Verle right behind her. The table is set with the good plates and two candles burning. Drew stands next to me with his arm on me like he's showing off a prize. "See, she's all in one piece. You didn't have to worry about a thing."

"And Grandma, look. I got straight-As again. See." I hand her my report card, but she doesn't take it.

"Well, you're not gonna get a A for that," Grandma says, pointing to the casserole I've made for dinner. It's more than a little brown on top. It's actually black in some spots, and it's runny—kind of like there's a puddle of water on top of the cheese crust. I think I put in too much milk.

Grandma laughs. "Oh Lordy be." She laughs some more. "Looks like I haven't taught you a thing."

"But y'all do look all cozy up in here playing house," Miss Verle says and laughs.

I never pay attention to Miss Verle, and Drew definitely doesn't. There's no use in talking to a drunk who's been drinking, which he figures she usually has because she smells like the contributions whether she comes in the morning or around suppertime. She smells like the contributions now.

"Come on. Grandma will show you how you treat a man. Not like that." Without ever looking at my report card, Grandma takes my hand and leads me to the kitchen.

Miss Verle follows two steps behind. "Drew," Grandma says real loud, "Miss Doris is fixin to put some hurtin to some chicken. I hope you'll stay."

"Miss Doris, you know I will."

JOHN BAILEY ASKED me why I lied to him about being in Jack & Jill. He said no one at Jack & Jill knew who I was. I never said I was in Jack & Jill; I just let him think I was. He says I probably lied about other things too. Like there's probably no reason for me to be saying no all the time when we're kissing. He says because my underwear is small and my shirts are so tight, I must have said yes before. He says he doesn't want to go with me anymore. Not unless he hears me say yes.

Drew's not used to me crying. No one is used to me crying. So when I show up at his job doing just that, he hugs me real tight and closes his office door.

"You want to talk about it?"

"John Bailey is stupid."

"I'm sure he is if he's responsible for making you feel this way."

"He's a fucker."

"No need to use that language." I love to be held so close.

"I'm not a kid. I'm sixteen. He's a stupid fucker." I talk directly into Drew's chest, and can feel my voice reverberate right back into me.

"Rachel, you're a young lady. You don't need to talk that way. Tell me what's going on. What'd he do?" Drew's still holding me tight with strong hands, steady. I think: Maybe Miss Verle saw the other day what I'm feeling now?

"No, it's me. I'm bad. You don't know. Really, I'm bad. You don't know how bad I can be . . ." Drew's arm around me is hot. It makes me hot.

You'd think that Sunday worship would make me good. At least that's what Grandma thought. Not every Sunday, but a lot of Sundays, there I'd be up in the AME Zion Church still singing like a white girl with not enough breath behind my notes. Maybe that's what mattered. That I didn't get the sounds right. I wasn't saying the right prayer. All I know is that being in Drew's arms—he's smart, and kind and understands the more sophisticated things like I do—it made me want to be close to him. Very close. I wanted him to stay. I wanted to find a way to keep him around. But I didn't pick the right way.

I remember him saying this before he leaned away from my kiss: "You're like a daughter to me. Go on home now."

THE NEXT DAY Tamika turns up and starts talking behind my back. Since sixth grade we've gone to the same school, and she has never liked me and I've never liked her. Her not liking me is on general principle. Me not liking her is because she still might beat me up. For the most part, I see her only in the hallways, sometimes near the bus stop after school. I'm in the honors classes and she's not.

She talks real loud as I stand in line for my free lunch. "She a ho. Think she all cute. She fast like those white girls. She slept with half the basketball team. She touch my man I'll slap her." She goes on and on. And people start laughing. And the part of me that wants to stop being sad, and to stop being hurt and not cry, turns around so quick—like I didn't even know myself—and says, "FUCK OFF," and punches Tamika so hard that she stumbles back. So hard that her nose bleeds.

"HEY, ALI," ANTHONY Miller calls out, on his way to his grandmother's. Since the fight with Tamika, Ali is me.

"How'd you get so brown?" he says.

I don't wear the sunscreen that Grandma tells me to. "Stay outta that sun. It'll make you dark and dusty," she says. I tell her that she is perpetuating racist ideas from slavery. There's nothing wrong with being dark-skinned. Like Drew says, I tell her: Black folks have to stick together. She doesn't like me to sass her. It's what her mother taught her and she's passing it on. But she hushes up then. The words "dark" and "dusty" only come out after she's had some of Miss Verle's contributions. She's not proud when she says those things.

"I like to tan," I say, my brown self reading a book on Grandma's porch rocking chair a couple of days into the summer break.

"It looks good on you," Anthony Miller says.

ANTHONY MILLER VISITS his grandmother every day that week and the next. Every day I see him, and we talk a little bit longer. I finish three books in ten days waiting on that porch. He never comes at the same time.

Somewhere around day eleven, Anthony Miller goes to visit his grandmother, and on his way back, I invite him inside.

The African brown fabric couch is covered with a milky plastic now. The pictures of faraway people Grandma's taken down long ago.

"Can we sit in your room? It's so hot. I think I'd stick to the couch." Anthony Miller smiles at me. He knows I'm the kind of girl who doesn't mind that kind of smile.

We go to my room. We kiss sitting up then lying down. I let Anthony Miller take off my shirt so that he can see what he's touching.

I want to be something. Some one thing. Maybe it is the it I was when Anthony Miller used to kiss me in the vestibule at Holy Redeemer.

Anthony Miller and I have never gone this far. That's such a strange thing to say. I never feel as if we're actually going anywhere.

"You're so beautiful. So beautiful." He says it over and over like it's a spell being cast over him. He closes his eyes. His hands are hungry to touch me. Whatever it is I am at this moment, it is something I want to be. But then the way Anthony Miller kisses me is fast. The way he touches me is hard. I feel like I'm going inside farther and farther the more he touches me.

When he touches me down there I count. He sticks his finger into me, and it feels like a pen jamming into a top. One. Two. Three. Four. Beautiful doesn't let it hurt.

Five. Six. "Please let me see what it feels like," he says. I feel his weight on me and his hands spreading my legs farther apart. Anthony Miller is taking the thing I thought I was giving. He is not big enough to make it impossible to fight back, but I don't. It's like my body thinks: surrender, beautiful. Seven. Eight. Nine.

"You are so beautiful," he says, and Grandma opens my bedroom door. She's not supposed to be at home. Maybe she heard his shoe fall to the floor, or the small noise I let out when he thrust harder to get deeper into me, dry.

She sees him and doesn't say "Stop" or "What are you doing?" She sees me and says, "You little hussy."

She doesn't yell or throw Anthony Miller out of the house half dressed. She doesn't do anything.

"I should have known," she says and then walks out of my room, closing the door behind her.

Anthony Miller pulls himself away. He pulls on his pants and shoes in a single move. I am lying on the bed still. My shirt is bunched around my right arm. My skirt is crowded around my middle. He doesn't need to hurry. Grandma isn't going to do anything. I'm getting what I deserve.

"Anyway, thanks," he says. Maybe he says something else.

Anthony Miller leaves without kissing me. He waves good-bye.

I hide the sheets from Grandma. I wash my hands and brush my teeth. I don't wash down there. I know I am bleeding.

THE NEXT DAY I go to the doctor by myself. I make a promise to myself: Never bring another boy to the house and meet my curfew each night. I am still a model student. I have straight As. I can still be something to be proud of: class vice-president, National Honor Society head, coeditor of the school's creative writing journal. I am a good student if not a good girl. Those are the things I will make count. The other things won't count. I can make things not count by writing them down any way I want.

In my diary, this is what I write:

"Having sex with Anthony Miller was quite an experience. Anthony Miller got kind of carried away and so did I. The doctor says I have a pretty bad tear down there. I should be more careful. And make sure I'm ready next time. I am still bleeding a little. I think he did something to me. I want him to do it again."

It's not a true story, but I tell it to myself. What difference does it make anyway? I tell myself that story because it could be true. It could have happened that way. Things happen in different ways.

Like that man, on the roof, maybe he tells himself stories the same way. Maybe his story goes like this: I saw the girl open the door (he waved at me); it was a whole family of folks (true too); I explained I was about to make a new roost—more birds—and the boy said he wanted to help (Robbie stuttered when he said p-p-p-please). They did their thing then. I did mine.

I don't know if the true story about Anthony Miller or about the day on the roof or about any story you could think of matters. If there's no one else to tell another side—the only story that can be told is the story that becomes true.

PART II

POETRY

Rachel

Heavy summer rain has drowned the few patches of grass that dared to grow in Grandma's backyard. All the vegetables and flowers Grandma used to grow have died. "There's nothing left to save," Grandma says over and over when she goes to see what's become of her garden after a few contributions. She's wrong. Wildflowers have taken root near the bird feeder I put out a few weeks ago. I guess they're not really wildflowers. They're wild sprouts, but they're green, and they're the only things growing in what used to be Grandma's garden.

Grandma doesn't like the bird feeder or the birds that it attracts. The other day she "nearly had a heart attack" with a knocking at her window in the morning. She thought a man was trying to break in. It was a black crow. Grandma wants me to take the bird feeder down to "keep flying vermin like that away." I won't. I like to hear the birds in the morning. I like to see that patch of green grow. "There's nothing left," Grandma says again when I tell her she's wrong about things not growing in the backyard. She doesn't listen. All her syllables are slurred.

Sometimes I hide her contributions. I empty out the bottles while she sleeps if anything is left in them. It's what Mor used to do with Pop's beer and cognac bottles. I know Miss Verle will stop by and bring Grandma another bottle of sherry within a day or so. It's still worth it.

There are some days Grandma doesn't get out of bed now that she's retired. Those days she drinks the contributions all day. She pours a bit of sherry to have after her coffee in the morning, and then with her tea in the afternoon. With her supper she drinks it straight while watching the evening news.

Seeing Grandma this way, it makes me know for certain that everything about a person will show up in another person in the family. I know the scientific way to talk about this: heredity and inheritances and the things that get passed on. But I think there should be a better explanation because Grandma never needed the contributions before Aunt Loretta died. But Pop needed them for a long time before. Heredity isn't supposed to work backward. I think about these things: the way that science or math tells us certain things. Math can explain the reason there's a one out of four chance that I'd have blue eyes. But it doesn't explain why me. And science or math can't explain what makes one person lucky, or what makes a person lucky enough to survive.

THREE WEEKS INTO summer and it feels like it will never end. The only good thing is that I don't have to see Anthony Miller or Tamika Washington or any of the other people from school. I spend my days at the library or on the porch rocking in Grandma's chair, reading. Grandma and me—we have different routines. We eat our meals separately. She talks on the phone. She visits with Miss Verle. She watches her stories on TV. There is a space between us bigger than the missing Aunt Loretta. We live in the same house but we both feel lonely. *We* and *lonely* don't belong in the same sentence.

"COME HERE, GRANDMA wants to show you something," Grandma says.

When Grandma talks to me, it is about God and the savior and how her days are short on God's earth. God is ever-present in our lives. He will lead the way. That kind of thing. She says I should get to the Lord. He's speaking to me now.

Grandma is maudlin. She talks about her death. How she wants to go down easy, like "a Texas afternoon iced tea." But there is nothing wrong with Grandma. She's not sick. She doesn't cough a lot or wheeze. She's almost seventy and takes the kind of pills old people on the evening news commercials talk about. But otherwise she seems fine except when the contributions catch up with her.

Today Grandma takes from her drawer a blue fabric Seagram's bag and dumps a collection of coins on her bedspread.

I draw my legs up and sit cross-legged on the bed before her. "Your penny collection?"

"Not just pennies," she says frowning. "Dimes. Nickels. John F. Kennedys."

Grandma picks up the newspaper next to her and opens it to a large advertisement that reads, "WE BUY COINS."

"You're going to the coin show?"

"But I can't see what's the years on them. Grandma's gonna make her some money before she dies. Better than my number coming in."

Grandma's number has never come in.

"Grandma you're not going to die."

"Not before I make a little money with this collection, for sure. But it's gonna happen."

"But the coins have to be very old to be worth something."

"Scoot up closer. Help Grandma see."

I haven't been this close to Grandma in a long time, and it makes me remember when I could lay in her lap and smell her lavender lotion.

"Here. Look at these," she says and pushes a pile of coins toward me on the bed.

"1977. 1964. 1980. They're not worth anything. You may as well spend them."

"Oh, no. I'm a collector. I should be having every year starting with 1935 and—see, I've got me a lot."

"Here's a good one. A nickel. From 1937. That's the year Pop was born."

"Let me see. How much could I get for that?"

I look at the newspaper ad. "For nickels from 1935 to 1943, it says five hundred dollars."

"Five hundred? Grandma's gonna be a rich old lady."

Grandma hasn't found the happy part of her voice in a long time—at least not around me. Then she's quiet for a long time. I sort the pennies from the nickels from the dimes and the John F. Kennedys. It's quiet in the house—a nice quiet—the kind you don't mind staying in.

"I talked to Drew about the troubles I've been having here with you," Grandma says after a while. "Troubles" means boys. "He thinks you just need to get involved in something that takes up your day better," she says. "He's got you a summer job at the center. Give you something to do." Grandma doesn't believe that I'm at the library when I say I am. There's no reason she should. "Lord, bless Drew," she says and I agree. "It's some other good mens out there—somewhere—I have to think."

Amen. That part's me. "When do I start?" I ask.

"Soon as you call him and tell him—tomorrow, the next day."

I jump from the bed to call Drew from the kitchen. I haven't seen him since that day. I have a second chance.

"Hey, we not through," Grandma yells. "Sit on back down."

I sit again but I am only partway there, double-checking each coin after Grandma inspects it with the black-handled, square magnifying glass. I am thinking of how I will impress Drew with what I wear, and how well I will do the work he assigns me. I think of how I will get him to like me—the way that I like him.

Grandma's collection is worth $2,507.03. "Make that two thousand. This one's for you. Same year as your daddy was born." We both get quiet as she hands me the nickel. It feels like we both have the same picture of him in mind. In mine, he is the way he was: handsome, smiling, posing in his blue uniform, five-stripes for the wing patches on his sleeve. In my mind, he is always in uniform. Handsome. Worthy of a salute.

"Is it bad to say—I think I won't always be able to remember him," I say.

"Oh, baby. That's your daddy," Grandma says.

"Why didn't Pop come back?" I ask.

"Some things are not to know, baby. I didn't have a daddy around growing up. And your daddy didn't neither. There's no mystery to that."

I study Grandma. I watch her close for hints and clues. She knows things she doesn't tell.

"I don't mean now. I mean then. When he called, he said he'd be there. He said he was on his way."

Grandma coughs and reaches for the contribution by her bed. Then she reaches for me and gives me a long hug.

"He said: 'Don't tell your mother. I'm coming to take you all home,' " I say. "And I didn't tell."

Grandma keeps holding on like she can wrap her arms around the words I'm saying and make them disappear. She rocks me back and forth; my head's on her shoulder. She strokes my hair along my back. She starts to hum.

"Your daddy could find his way around anyplace. Did you know that? He made maps but that was for other folks. Lord, have mercy. I remember the time I took him and your Aunt Loretta out to the campgrounds with the church. He was seven years old. Not two minutes into being there had he done run off. He was looking for the horses he'd seen on the road coming in. It was the dead of night before he come back to find us. Him finding us! Not afraid of the dark. Not afraid of being lost. He walked up to the campfire like he was walking into that very living room there," she says and points. "And he said: Mama, they let me feed that horse. What a whipping he got that night," she says and laughs.

"What I'm saying, baby, is that your daddy could find whatever he's looking for. He knows how. Some thing's best not found."

Grandma holds me tighter then like she wants to keep all my questions inside.

"Your daddy, Rachel. Bury him, baby. In your heart, and your mind. It's no point—the holding on."

Her voice is so soft it's like she's whispering this to herself.

"But, what if he was on his way when he said?"

"No more questions."

"But, what if he did come?"

"Oh baby, he did. He just came too late that day."

Rachel

"You smell like marzipan," Jesse says when he shakes my hand hello.

It's my first day as an intern at the Salvation Army Harbor Lights Center. I'm wearing a blazer, a button-down silk shirt, a skirt, and high-heeled shoes like Aunt Loretta used to wear.

"Jesse's our other intern," Drew says. "Rachel's my surrogate niece, but really like a daughter to me."

Again he says it—"like a daughter"—the way he did that day. This time it sounds like a warning in secret code.

Jesse is tall and made of right angles only. He has a square jaw and a sharp clean line for a nose. He has blond hair and sea green eyes. "You smell like marzipan" isn't a common thing to say when you meet someone.

"Hi," I say. "Marzipan was one of my favorite things when I was a kid."

"Me too. My mom—she's from Norway—she used to make it when I was little," Jesse says.

"From there as in *from* there?" I ask.

"From just outside Oslo."

"Drew, did you know that?" I ask.

"I didn't," he says. "But I don't come in here smelling like marzipan either." Drew laughs. For a moment I think Drew has been paying attention to me, to the way I look, to the perfume I'm wearing, to the way that I am not his daughter.

"My mom was Danish," I say.

"Really?"

His "really" feels like a challenge for some reason, and I find sounds within me I have not used in years: "*Taler du norsk?*"

"I'm fine. Wait—how do you say that again? I am fine."

"In Danish you say, '*Jeg har det godt.*'" Where have these sounds come from?

"You speak Norwegian too?" Jesse asks.

"I think I could probably understand it. The main difference is the intonation. And spelling. And some words."

"Okay, but did you ask me how I was?" Jesse asks.

"Nope."

"Busted. Mom never got around to teaching us the language," he says. "I don't think it's gonna stick now." He says "Mom" and laughs at himself with a voice that is not at all white-guy sounding. It's not the words he says, but his voice— it has the texture of Deacon James's when he preaches, the feel of Drew's when he speaks.

"Jesse can show you where you're sitting, and between the two of you decide how to split up the work. Jesse knows what needs to get done."

"And Rachel," Drew says. "Good news," though I don't understand why I should think it is once he tells me: "Lakeisha's coming to visit next week for the summer. She's looking forward to seeing you."

JESSE'S GOING TO be a freshman at Reed College in the fall. He lives across the Fremont Bridge over in the Northwest hills. He went to Catlin Gabel, a private school. That means he's probably rich. I wonder why someone like him would want to be somewhere like here. Especially if you didn't have to be. The center is not exactly dirty, but it's not new. And the men who are in the rehab program here can be kind of scary. Some have lived on the street for years. For most of them it shows: They have black teeth and deep lines in their faces; they have heavy cigarette coughs and rough skin.

The good thing about the center is that even though it feels poor there's also a feeling of hope. The men joke with each other and laugh. They drink lots of coffee and work hard at the jobs they've been assigned. They all want to get better.

"It looked good on my college applications. It's not the kind of thing I want to do for real, but it's an easy job," Jesse says when I ask. He's nonchalant when he says it. He makes a crooked grin.

"Why are you here?" he asks me.

I don't mention Anthony Miller or the plan Grandma and Drew have for me. "Same."

Above Jesse's desk are two pictures of his family—mom, dad, and sister.

"We went to Denmark last year," Jesse says, pointing to the photo of his family standing next to a guard at the queen's castle.

I have never thought of Denmark as a landscape. Denmark, the one I know, has never been so much a real place as a story setting for things that Mor did or told. I know Denmark through her stories. My Denmark would be pictures of bakeries full of fresh bread, school rooms with desks that open like a box, and Christmas trees decorated with real candles. In the pictures of my Denmark there wouldn't be people—except for Mor, except for the times I put myself there too. If I had drawn a picture of Denmark, it would have been a picture of a feeling inside me, I think—like a cloudless sky, somewhere close to the color blue.

"My mom would trip out if you talked Danish to her," he says. "That'd be cool."

AT A QUARTER after twelve, I'm not close to halfway through the pile of papers I'm supposed to file by the end of the day. Jesse and I have been talking the whole time.

Jesse isn't like a white guy. He calls white people pilgrims. He speaks a broken Mayan Spanish. He recites revolutionary Jamaican poems by heart. He's surprised that I haven't read *Black Skin, White Masks* all the way through.

Jesse lived in New York City until he was twelve. He spent long holidays and summers in Jamaica and the Virgin Islands. His family has homes in all of those places. Jesse is a vegetarian and knows things about black people that only black people know—like what it means for a black girl's hair to "go back." The things I learned after I came to live with Grandma and Aunt Loretta. I'm surprised that someone would have told him. Had he actually asked?

I HEAR THE music even before we reach the recreation room. It's not a song I know, but a part of me wants to fill in words to each note. It's a sad song, but also one with hope. In the recreation room, there's a man playing piano and a few men watching TV. It feels like a waiting room more than a recreation room. The couches and chairs are shallow and are made of a rough-looking red canvas material. The floor has no rugs. The television, mounted high in the corner like in a doctor's office, is barely twenty inches across and must be difficult to see with the light that cuts in from the bare window. It is only the piano music that makes it feel like a place you'd want to relax.

Jesse and I sit and eat silently, both listening to the music.

When the piano player finishes, one guy claps. Jesse and I clap too. The piano player gets up and hugs Jesse, and they pat each other on the shoulder the way that black men would with closed fists. How does Jesse know this too?

"Yo, man. Time to get back to work," the piano player says.

"This is Drew's niece."

"She's a pretty young lady."

I smile.

"Are you a model? You've got beautiful eyes," the piano player says.

"No."

"My man, ain't got any manners," Jesse says. "The brother grew up in the Chicago projects."

"Lived in the projects and the streets. I grew up when I got here," the piano player says.

The piano player is tall. I have to tilt my head up sixty degrees to look at his face. He is nice-looking. Not handsome, but pretty. He has his mother's eyes, I think. He has a way of seeing that his mother gave him is what I mean. It is my first thought. Then I notice the color (brown with gold flecks) and the (long) lashes. He has a deep soulful gaze and a way of seeing into you.

"How tall are you? Do you mind me asking?" I say.

"Just shy of six five."

"Almost six and a half feet?"

"Yeah, and I never played ball."

"You get this all the time," I say.

"Like you hear, where are you from? When they want to know where you got those beautiful eyes." I am charmed so easily. I hope it doesn't show. "From my aunt. Aunt Loretta," I say.

"Slow your roll, dawg," Jesse says.

I smile.

"There's nothing wrong with complimenting a young lady."

"This is my buddy. He's good people," Jesse says. "A star in the program."

"You're in the program?" I ask.

"I was. Got 120 days clean now. Your uncle hired me on staff when I finished—at least until I find something more permanent. You here for the summer?" the piano player asks.

"I'm working here for the summer. For Drew. I mean. And I'm from here, but," and I say for no particular reason, "I used to live in Chicago too."

"Chi-town in the house, right?" The piano player puts out his fist for me to touch.

"Yeah." I am embarrassed because I don't know what to do. Do I knock his fist with my own? Hold out my hand, palm flat?

He must see the discomfort in my eyes.

"Let me do this proper." He takes my hand gently in his own and kisses it. "Hi, my friends call me Brick."

Brick

Brick was used to the small squat building. It was not used to his frame. He hunched beneath the showerhead to wash his hair. He could have guessed that he would be this tall. No one else—if anyone had been paying attention—would have made the same prediction since he had been so small for his age as a boy.

He rented this spare room five blocks away from the Salvation Army Harbor Lights Center. It was all the world he could handle after roaming the country for the last six years; he knew what kind of landscape he belonged in.

The first months after he left home—before the pimples showed up on his chin, and the hair appeared in his armpits and on his below parts, before his voice began to deepen—he spent with the white man and woman he came to know as Paul and Lisa.

They'd stand on the side of the road near freeway ramps. "Will play song for money. Help us and our kid."

The cardboard box sign and the fact that they placed themselves at a traffic light worked. On most days they'd collect enough to eat, to pay for a place to sleep, and to get high. Not many folks asked for the song. But when they did, you could be sure they'd add a five- or a ten- or a twenty-dollar bill to the spare change they had first placed in Lisa's hand with pity or contempt or disgust. "You really shouldn't have your boy out here—out of school," came the familiar rebuke. It was funny: No one ever questioned the veracity of their family. Brick didn't know how people made sense of the two young rockers with a curly-haired, light brown boy in tow. But they did. And no one ever thought to ask Brick: Do you want to stay with your mom and dad? Or would you like to live in a real home?

Paul and Lisa didn't treat him too badly. They didn't beat him; they fed him when they ate; gave him a place to sleep each night they had one. And on the nights he woke screaming with the bird-boy's face in his mind's eye or the pigeon man chasing him in his dreams, they gave him that melty-feeling pill to make the bad dreams disappear.

There were a couple of times, though—of course it was only when they were high and drunk—they thought it was funny when his sex got hard. Once he ejaculated while the woman named Lisa toyed with him. He was so scared of having that thing sneeze again for a week he was afraid to touch it when he peed.

As the months passed, he grew. His monkey face must have looked suddenly more menacing. He was as tall as a high school senior by age twelve. He was a black boy and no use to Paul and Lisa, who needed not just a good musician but a child to make their panhandling a success.

They left him one afternoon. It'd been raining for three days in a row and they scored no more than a few bucks in change after twelve-hour shifts. Irritable, totally not high, Paul and Lisa left their monkey and the bill at the diner where they had a late lunch. One monkey wasn't going to stop their show.

That was the first of a series of adoptions for Brick. That night it was the waitress—fifty-something, a mother whose son had been jailed for killing a man—who took him home. She wanted him to shut the blinds for her. Check around the house. She hadn't known how much she needed a man around to feel safe until her son was sent away. Brick stayed there for two weeks until the day she called the family services to get him a real place to live. He wrote thank you on a pad by the phone, and left without the sandwich she'd made him for lunch. The one thing he was certain of—even at that young age—was that he'd find his own home.

Next there was the old man: a blind army vet who needed help with the yard and some things around the house. "Niggers changed everything around this neighborhood." He couldn't hear the black in Brick's voice. He shared his theories about spooks with Brick for a week until Brick could take it no longer. Then there was the piano teacher, a widow, who heard Brick play his harmonica at the bus stop and invited him home to hear her play. She played him a beautiful waltz and gestured for him to sit on the bench so she could show him. It was the first time he had played a piano and though his hands were unsteady at first, he caught on quickly. He was a natural, the woman said. They had a cozy routine after that: breakfast, a morning walk, a little gardening, to the grocery store, home to the piano—a song and a lesson, an afternoon nap and supper by six. The widow drew him into her day as if it were the most natural thing in the world, as if she had been living with a sky with no sun. He was there four months when her kids got wind of him staying there and called the cops. "Little con artist" they called him and claimed Brick was trying to muscle in on their inheritance.

The list went on and on: the single mom with a six-month-old son, the retired Jewish couple with the would-be show dog, the black man with three old Chevys on cement blocks in his driveway. These people would take him in for a spell. He'd help around the house or do work in the yard—he'd do whatever he could to earn the right to another meal and a night's sleep indoors. He drifted for months, living on the kindness of strangers. Brick was boyish despite his size, and he charmed everyone he met. But by the time he turned fifteen, things began to change. Because of his size he looked much older than he was—like a man who could be thirty. A drifter—no matter his magazine-friendly face—was likely to be a gang member, a drug dealer, something that brought trouble.

Homes were closed to him. And he became a man of his own then.

He did odd jobs here and there. Kitchen help. Moving man. Stockroom boy. Ranch hand.

At night he'd frequent the town bar, have a beer—always too much beer. But he wasn't an alcoholic, which was what he'd told himself on the mornings he couldn't remember how he had found himself to this or that motel or rented room.

He went through as many names as he did towns. Monkey. Slim. T.J. People were always giving him a letter for a name. In one town he was D2 for a stretch—every stranger at the bar got the name Dee—he just happened to be the second stranger to appear in one day.

Never did he think of going home. Was home still there? Was it ever?

He wondered often about his mother. Fixed in his mind, was an image of his best her. She was smiling, seated on the old green couch when it was new, still plastic-wrapped and clean, with him on her lap. He was five, maybe six. She was tickling him with the long braid she'd made of her hair, and he was tickling back. Who took that photograph? He didn't know. But it always made him feel hopeful. There was a witness to those good days; another person who knew his mother's best her.

Brick continued to play the harmonica, and in the bars he'd play the piano. He'd start with something rousing, a good bar song—and always, always he'd end the night with Roger's song.

Women loved him. He was big now; he had a wide, solid back, lean through the middle, forearms strong with Indian hair, and his chest too. His teeth, an inheritance—the best legacy of years of ancestors bred in slavery, he'd say wryly—were straight and solid. God, when he smiled at the girls! And when he played his music—what they wouldn't do—but that was not what made him play.

"I like that song," the women would say. "The one at the end. What are the words?" There were no words. But when a girl would ask, he'd make up some lyrics. Hum. Mmmm. Hmmm. Hum. The words were sometimes just a jumble of unrelated phrases—all related to Roger's story, the one he repeated to himself each night. Still promising himself one day he'd continue his journey. Always the reminder of the birdboy's face, his promise to Roger, his now missing childhood. And always the girls had questions: "How'd you end up here?" Meaning Saint Louis, Oak Falls, Minneapolis, Saint Paul, Fargo, Tucson, Sheridan, Phoenix, Banner—small town or city. "What brought you here?" I had to run from the police, age eleven—because I was wrongly accused. "Of what?" Not being able to see what was right before my eyes. And then of lying about it.

HE ARRIVED IN Portland about six months ago with a bad case of the shakes. Five days into his own personal detox that he rode through on a bus. In Portland he wandered around Union Station trying to get someone to help him. It wasn't easy to get people even to look at him: a tall man, shaking, unshaven, three days past his last shower.

Drew happened to be in the bus station that day—his weekly effort to round up more folks, get the men and women off the street. He brought a bag of literature about the Salvation Army's rehab program and a bag of fresh sandwiches.

"I can help maybe," Drew said when he saw Brick. "Here, have a sandwich."

"Thanks. No. I need real help."

"Tell me, son."

He hadn't been a son for so long. "I gotta get this—I gotta get through this. I can't do it any more."

"Come with me down to the Harbor Lights Center. We can talk about how you can do this one day at a time."

Brick knew he was too young to go to the center, so when they asked he said he was twenty-five. Brick wanted to get a fresh start—go where he could beat this thing.

He'd been at the center ever since. First as a patient—ninety days of rehab—and now as a janitor.

It was a hot summer day, and he couldn't cool down from his steamy shower. He went to the window and opened it. The air was still, and the summer air entered the apartment in a fresh spray. Brick's apartment window looked out onto a courtyard as it did when he was a child. Below his window was a grilling area. To the far right he could see a swing and a sandbox. He could hear the children playing tag. He wanted to be closer to their laughter. He liked having the outside sounds in.

He'd been out of breath all day since he met her at the center earlier. The fuzzy-haired girl with the blue blue eyes was now a young woman. He shouldn't be surprised that he'd found her. After all the years he imagined meeting her, he had not imagined this. When did he know it was her? He couldn't be sure. He should have known as soon as he looked in her eyes, or when she mentioned Chicago. No. It was when he took her hand in his, held it to his lips, pressed his lips against her hand, and she squeezed back.

Rachel

The whole summer, the whole look of my life is starting to change.

Jesse and I go to lunch together every day. Sometimes after work we walk down the street to the bookstore and hang out at the cafe. Jesse has me reading books and writers I never thought about reading: Carlos Castaneda, Amiri Baraka, and two books on capitalism. Jesse reads on both sides of every issue.

It's strange doing these kinds of things with a boy. I never really thought of boys as people to talk to. Jesse asks me questions about what I like and what I want in my life. And it's like I don't have to worry about being a girl around him.

Sometimes Brick hangs out with us too. Jesse is tutoring him for his GED. Brick never finished school but wants to start at the community college in the fall.

When Jesse and Brick talk, I can forget that Jesse's white, and I can forget that Brick's black. Or Brick's something like that. I don't ask Brick what he is. Brick is light-skinned with golden colors in his brown eyes. He could be black or Mexican or mixed like me. He's twenty-five and maybe at that age it doesn't matter.

When I hang out with Jesse and Brick at lunch and sometimes after work, we talk about the people who walk through Pioneer Courthouse Square or real things: like what's happening in the world, or books, or things like that. I forget that what you are—being black or being white—matters. Jesse makes me see there's a different way to be white. And Brick makes me see there's a different way to be black.

But I do tease Jesse about being Norwegian. Sometimes I think he just made it up.

"My middle name's Gustav—shouldn't that be proof enough?" Jesse says.

"Not really," I say.

"Okay, wait until you meet my mom. You'll see how Norwegian I am. Just because I can't speak it . . ." His voice trails off.

"How do you say be careful?" he says finally.

"In Norwegian? I don't know."

"I think something like, *Ha det bra,*" Jesse says. "My mom would always say that. Like if we were about to touch something that would burn, or we'd be running in the house and she was afraid we'd trip and fall. It was like that was the one thing she couldn't say fast enough in English when we were little."

"In Danish, you'd say *pas på.* My mom used to say that all the time too."

"HEJ," JESSE'S MOTHER says when she greets me at the door. She's slightly shorter than Jesse. She has curly blond hair that goes to her shoulders. She has lines that crinkle at the edges of her green eyes.

"Rachel speaks Danish, mom," Jesse says, and gives me a poke in the side as my cue.

"*Det er godt—*" I stammer but don't know how to finish the sentence. I was never pleased to meet someone as a kid. How do I say: "I am pleased to meet you"?

Jesse's mom looks at Jesse and then says in English with not even a little bit of an accent, "How glad I am you brought her. Welcome and come in."

She steers me to the dining room where the table is decorated something like Mor would decorate for a special occasion: white tea lights burning, cloth napkins, and the special blue and white china. "I've made a traditional Scandinavian dinner. I hope you'll like it. It's good to make it for someone who appreciates it."

"Mom, you know I'm a vegetarian now. I can't eat that meatball stuff," Jesse says.

"I can't wait," I say.

The smell of familiar food fills the house. It smells like *frikadeller* or *fleskestej*? *Kartoffler* or *ris*? I don't know whether I'm imagining those things, but Jesse's mom promises she's made a real apple cake for dessert. "Of course, it's not like my mom's," she says.

"But we have lots of food. I hope you're hungry," she says and points at the dishes that are already on the table. "There's red cabbage."

"*Rødkål*," I say translating; it's a Danish food too.

"And potatoes."

"*Kartoffler*."

And then it becomes a game. Jesse's mom points at the beans. "*Bønner.*" Beets. "*Rødbeder.*" Cucumber salad. "*Aguker salat.*"

If only I could turn the corner and find Mor right there in the kitchen. Smiling, happy. Robbie would be at the table reading his *Anders And* comic books for at least the third time. I'd sit there with him, reading my book too. Pop getting home from work would be the day's celebration. And we'd eat.

JESSE GIVES ME a tour of his house. There are five bedrooms, four bathrooms, a deck with a grill that you plug in, and a swimming pool. All the furniture looks new even though there is no plastic on it. This is what it feels like to be rich, I think. You have nice things, but you don't worry about them.

Jesse's dad comes home about twenty minutes later. Jesse's sister's going to stay at a friend's. She doesn't like Scandinavian food.

"Shall we sit?" Jesse's father says, and we do.

He pours wine into the glasses already set on the table. For his wife, first; then for me and Jesse he pours more than just a taste; and then he pours a full glass for himself. "*Skål!*" he says raising his glass.

"*Skål!*" And even though I've never done it before, I sip my wine after I raise my glass. Just a sip. I don't want heredity to start working on me.

"DOESN'T SHE SPEAK Danish so well?" Jesse's mom says even though I've been quiet most of the meal.

"I wouldn't know, honey. I don't speak the language. And as I recall, neither do you," his father says.

"I wish that I had taught the kids Norwegian. It's impressive that she can remember a language she hardly uses. Rachel," she says turning to me, "what's that?" She's pointing at a bookshelf. "Do you remember how to say that?"

"*Boghylde.*"

"And this?" She's pointing to the table.

"*Bord.*" The faster I answer the better.

"And that?"

"*Vindue.*" Window. She doesn't want me to speak in complete sentences.

"Amazing," she says.

"Ma'am," I say. "You speak really well too."

Jesse laughs.

"I mean, you don't seem to have an accent," I say. "My mom did. I mean I didn't really hear it, but other people said she did."

"Well, in truth, I was a baby when I came to the United States, right after the war. I'm more American than Norwegian. Sometimes it feels like being Norwegian was just a part of my childhood—like my favorite overalls or buckteeth or skinned knees," she says.

I don't want being Danish to be something that I can put on and take off. I don't want the Danish in me to be something time makes me leave behind.

JESSE DRIVES ME home, and I try to say good night in the car. But he's a gentleman and insists on walking me to the door. Grandma shouldn't see me come home with a boy. I hope she's in bed, but I can see the lights are on.

"Okay, bye," I say to Jesse at the door.

"Bye," he says.

"Rachel?" Grandma's calling me. "Who's that with you?"

"Nobody."

"Tell him to come in."

It's embarrassing to say what happens next. Jesse follows me in, and we both see a tangle of naked bodies on the screen—men and women on a scratchy videotape Grandma is playing.

"You understand this?" she says addressing Jesse and pointing to the screen. Not hello. Or tell me your name. Or anything polite and regular. "All them folks have mamas. How come they get raised up like that?" A full bottle of contribution stands empty beside her. It's the second in two days.

"Ma'am?" Jesse says. But he can't help but laugh.

"I'm serious, now. Don't it matter what your mama do?"

The tape keeps playing and Grandma turns up the volume. "Ain't this something though," she says. "Glad to know what the fuss is all about."

"Where'd you get that tape, Mrs. Morse?" He's still laughing.

"Miss Verle gave it to me with Mr. Donahue on it. Now all of a sudden this come up."

"Miss Verle is a nasty lady," Jesse says.

Grandma looks at him close for a moment. And then starts to laugh. "She sho is. She is." They laugh together.

It's late and finally I say good-bye to Jesse. He tells Grandma how his mother has invited me over again—Grandma's welcome to come next time too.

"Well, that'd be nice. Haven't had a white woman cook for me in years." And they both start to laugh again.

"It would be a pleasure to have you come next time, ma'am."

"Now, that's a young man with manners," Grandma says as she closes the door behind him.

WE'RE HAVING A welcome back dinner for Lakeisha. Grandma's not feeling well. She had promised to make dinner, but when I got home she was a full bottle of contributions into the day. I told Drew she had a cold, so instead he's taken us to his favorite restaurant downtown.

Lakeisha wears contacts now. She's grown a little bit taller and a little bit fatter. But she's not fat. Lakeisha is not much of a talker unless you're talking about hair and makeup (she's going to cosmetology school) or boys. So Lakeisha doesn't say much as we eat, because Drew wants to talk about the day's news (an antiapartheid demonstration the other day), the book about affirmative action he just read, and tennis. I have been reading the newspaper, the *New York Times*, since Jesse started bringing it to me from home. I know about everything that Drew is talking about. It's on my mind too.

"You're so quiet tonight, Lakeisha," Drew says as we eat the restaurant's special pie, not cobbler but a good pecan kind.

"Why you have to talk about things that are so boring?" Lakeisha says.

"What's not boring?"

"I don't know," she says.

"I'll tell you what's not boring. Seeing somebody get on the right track. There's a new kid at the center," Drew says. "A good kid. It's been exciting to see him turn it all around." Drew calls everyone a kid. Even someone like me.

Lakeisha is not interested in what Drew does. She yawns when he talks about how important it is to give back. When she met us at the center, she said to me, "You like working with a bunch of bums too?" She tells people her dad works at a hospital. She says it's nasty thinking about her dad being around bums all the time.

"You mean Brick," I say.

"We hired him on. He's a hard worker. I'd love to see him do something more. Stay clean. He's talented. A musician too. A nice young man."

"Ooo, he that tall one. He fine," Lakeisha says. Now she's interested. We're talking about boys. "I saw him when I was coming in."

"He's too old for you. Plus, he's one of those bums," I say teasing her. I don't mean that. Brick is a nice guy. And he is very nice-looking, but I don't think of him that way. I don't know why.

"They're not bums. They're recovering alcoholics and addicts," Drew says.

"It's all creepy up in there. I don't like it. It smells."

"Then it's good you don't work there," I say.

"Then it's good you don't work there," Lakeisha says with a high voice and her best white people accent.

LAKEISHA AND I wait for Drew in the car while he goes back to get the jacket he left in the restaurant booth.

Lakeisha turns around to say, "You like the white boy, huh? The one sit by you?"

I don't say anything.

"I saw you all up close and talking when I walked in. You can have him. I don't know nothing about no white boys. But I don't know why you'd want that when that fine tall boy's there."

"Jesse's just a friend. And we work together."

I haven't really thought about Jesse this way. It's like I've been feeling that the part of me that is a girl is invisible to him. White guys don't notice black girls, and black girls don't look at white guys that way. But when I think about it again, maybe Jesse does like me. Maybe I like him.

"Girl, he ain't thinkin friend when he looks at them titties. Me, I want that fine tall one," Lakeisha says, ignoring me. "I don't usually like them light-skinned-ed but he look good."

"He's twenty-five. He's too old for you," I say again.

"No he not. I need a real man."

"I thought you wanted a man with a job?"

"He got a job. But he gonna have to get one better to take care of the things I like. You say something to him okay? And I promise not to say anything to the white boy."

"Why should I care if you say anything to Jesse? It isn't true."

"You like a white boy. You like a white boy," she says in singsong until Drew opens the car door.

Brick

For weeks Brick wondered how to approach Rachel—how to tell the story he'd promised to tell. He often joined her for lunch with Jesse. They would each get a slice of pizza or a sandwich at the deli and then eat in Pioneer Courthouse Square watching people go by.

Rachel never talked about herself. When Brick asked her where she lived in Chicago, she said she couldn't remember. The way she shut off—her eyes went blank; her voice went low—he knew Chicago wasn't a memory she visited often. He would have to find the right moment to tell her the story he'd promised Roger he'd share.

Today he had promised Drew to deliver a box to Rachel's grandmother. He hoped Rachel would be home.

Brick took a shower that was extra long this morning. He didn't mind when the water started to run cold—he was still shaping his thoughts.

My name's Brick. But it used to be something else. I used to live downstairs from you. In Chicago. I met your dad and he said tell you this.

Brick felt lucky. He was going to tell her a story. It was a story that would help her make sense of things that maybe didn't make sense, of those Chicago memories.

The water was running very cold. He was still smiling. He was a shiny coin in fountain water. He was going to make wishes come true.

RACHEL LOOKED SLIGHTLY scared when she opened the door, he thought, or maybe it was just a look of surprise. Her bright blue eyes seemed a little wet. She hid her body behind the front door.

"Hi," he said.

"Hi."

"Drew asked me to drop this off for your grandmother." He made the box, which was filled with papers and letters, look heavier than it was. "Where can I put it?"

She ushered him in. "Over there," she said, pointing to the table.

"You scared me. I didn't really expect a person—," she said. "I was feeding the birds earlier, and they sometimes come looking for more."

"And they knock on the door?"

"No they ring the bell. Duh!" she said, but she was smiling

and Brick didn't feel so stupid for his question. He was just so nervous. He didn't really know what to say.

"They peck at the window. It can sound like a knock," she said.

"Oh," he said and tried to laugh along with her.

Rachel looked beautiful. She was wearing a pale blue summer dress he'd seen her wear at the center before. Her eyes in the summer light were bright as headlights.

Brick set the box down on the table and then suddenly didn't know what to do with his hands. He was too tall, too clumsy, too awkward, too tongue-tied to manage words. He'd never been alone with her before.

His eyes fixed on the photos on the mantel. "Is this your father? I can see the resemblance."

"Really?"

"Through the nose, mouth." And, he thought, the way that I am touched by you.

"I don't remember him much," she said. "I mean I miss him. But he kind of left us," she continued. "I mean me. So then Grandma got me. I came to live with her."

He didn't have to ask about her mother. "I'm sorry," he said instead of *Let me explain. Your father said you would be safer here. And this is why.*

"Who's this?" he asked, holding a photograph of a young woman.

"My Aunt Loretta."

This time it wasn't fear, but sadness, that registered in Rachel's face. Brick studied the picture. The woman had a pageboy hairdo and pearl earrings and a necklace to match, and the same soft jawline and high cheekbones as her niece. They did not have the same color eyes.

"You must have your mom's eyes," he said.

Rachel took the photograph from him when he looked up at her again as if comparing. She wiped dust from the frame.

He realized he was going too fast. You couldn't fill a room with ghosts when you didn't know what power they might have.

"Is your grandmother home?" he asked.

"Yeah, she's asleep. Otherwise I wouldn't be allowed to let you in. Do you want to wait for her?"

"Umm . . ."

"Oh. It'd be okay. The rule is no boys allowed in the house. But maybe you don't count as a boy since—well, you're older."

"Oh."

Brick sat. His legs were impossibly long. Impossible because he could not figure how to cross them or lean them to the side without looking effeminate. He was a pretty man so he lowered his voice when he talked; he made sure to stand straight. He put his hands in his pockets. In those ways, he thought, he made himself look more manly. "You're so pretty," the women would say. "How do I know you're not gay?" That's what the women would tease him with. His beauty. He had learned that the women who said this wanted him to be rough with them—take them in his arms hard. He'd done it a couple of times—both drunk and high—but not without the uneasy feeling that claimed his throat and his gut later. He'd hold the women the way the bruising hands of the pigeon man had held him. It was not the touch he wanted or wanted to give.

"So do you like the job at the center?" He folded his hands in his lap. Slow, slowly.

"Yeah, I like it," she said, fanning the pages of a thick book. "Otherwise I'd be here reading the whole summer. I think I could read the whole library through."

Without Jesse between them, Brick felt uncomfortable in her presence. Boyish. Usually their conversations were so easy. He was all nerves now and filled the silence with questions.

You like reading?

What's your favorite book?

And how come?

What's the biggest book you ever read?

He asked her what was her favorite food, color, day of the week, holiday?

She answered his questions then said, "That's not a way to know people."

There was a long silence. Then Brick heard a toilet flush at the back of the house.

"I think she's up." Rachel looked toward a closed door. Silence. The remote control clicked. The television turned on. "I think she's gonna watch her story. Yeah, you better not disturb her now."

Again, they were quiet.

If he wasn't going to tell her Roger's story, then he should leave.

I'm Jamie. I used to live downstairs. He couldn't form the words. Today maybe wasn't the day. He felt rubbed down — dull.

He was about to stand to go when she said, "Hey."

"Yeah?"

"So, can I ask you a question?" she asked. "You had so many for me."

"Yeah, sure . . ." Did she know the reason he'd come? Did she recognize who he was?

"What are you?" she asked.

"What do you mean?"

"You're from Chicago. But what are you? Like black, or — like me?"

"Oh, I'm black. Regular." He said "regular" like he was describing coffee without milk. "Normal," he said amending his answer. "Just black."

"I didn't mean . . ." she said.

"That's okay," he said, trying to take out whatever edge he had in his words. "I don't mind. Really." And then, "Do you think people would ask you that if you didn't have your mother's eyes?"

"I don't know," she said and her voice changed. When he looked at her, he saw a building, her brother, a fall. There was actual sky in her eyes. He wanted to take it back — put the question back inside.

"Hey, can we go outside?" he said. "I want to see that bird feeder."

"Really?" she asked.

"I used to know something about birds," he said. "A long time ago."

IN THE BACKYARD Rachel propped herself on the gate. Brick took a seat on a stump.

"Did you meet Drew's daughter, Lakeisha?" Rachel asked.

"Yeah."

"She likes you."

"Oh?"

"She's eighteen."

"Oh."

"I told her that if you and me and Jesse go somewhere. She could come."

"Sure."

A bird flew down from the neighbor's walnut tree. It pecked at the bird feeder, then flew off. "It got so close," Rachel said. "How come?"

"I guess we didn't scare it."

"I know that. I meant you said you knew a lot about birds. Was this something that kind of bird normally does?"

"I don't know. I knew what they looked like, and I remembered their songs. Not so much what they did and stuff."

"Is that what you wanted to do? Before . . ."

Before he became a bum, Brick knew she was thinking. Before he was an addict, an alcoholic, someone who had lived on the street.

"An ornithologist," she said.

"Big word."

"I like big words," she said.

"I never thought of liking words," he said.

"What do you like? Best? I bet I could guess," she said. "Music."

"You're right," he said, and he took out his harmonica, the silver harmonica that was Roger's gift.

"You play that? Too?" she asked. "That's weird. That you would play that."

"Weird? It's a way to make music out of a whistle," Brick said. "Like a bird does. Let me show you." With his cupped hands around the instrument, with his eyes closed, he played Roger's song.

"It's a song I knew once. Now I think it's a song I made up," he said.

"What do you call it?" she asked.

"I don't know."

"It needs a title. I think I'd call it 'Flight.' "

How would he say what he had to say?

Instead he said, "I'm not twenty-five. I'm seventeen. I lied so I could get in the center. I didn't want to end up in foster care. I ran away. I was eleven. I kind of lived with anyone who would take me in for years. I mean, I say ran away but I thought I was going to something. I just kind of lost my way at some point."

"Where were you going?"

"Right here, I guess. I guess I was going right here. Don't they always say that you end up exactly where you're supposed to be?"

"Do you miss home?" she asked.

He shrugged. Missing people, missing home. He hadn't allowed himself a feeling like that in so long. "I did so many different things when I lived on the road: ranch hand, factory worker, piano player in a bar. I don't think I missed out on much. Even if it wasn't a proper growing up, I think I had a lot of growing up experiences."

"Except," and unable to explain why roller coasters and cotton candy, roasted peanuts and Ferris wheels were suddenly on his mind, he said, "an amusement park. I never got to go on one of those rides." He felt young around her—back to his own age—and maybe younger. He missed out on the chance to seek out a fright just for fun.

"I was small for my age. If you can believe it. I was never tall enough to get on the big rides as a kid," he said.

"That's easy then," she said. "We'll pick a day and we'll go. I used to love amusement parks. There's Oaks Park. It's not Disneyland, but . . . it's closer."

"Okay," he says. "Okay." Okay, he thought, it's a date.

"Next week. Next Saturday?"

"Sure. Yeah, okay."

They sat silently watching the birds come and go. They were common birds: sparrows, robins, and the occasional large crow. Brick put his hands back in his pockets now, afraid of the silence. But certain today he would not tell.

"I won't tell your secret. That's a promise," she said. "I'm good at not telling."

Nella

Day 766. I don't know what to do. Why did he do it? Anything could have happened. When I came home from work there was just Doug on the couch watching TV. When I said where are the kids, he said he took them to the park. He said they wanted to go. I know they wanted to go but they can't go alone. They can't be alone out there. They don't know this place. He said he told them how to get home. He showed them the way. I can't believe he took them out and left them there. I went to take them home. They were right there when I walked out. I hugged them to me. I think Robbie was scared because he saw me crying. I was so happy they were okay. My babies were okay. What if something happened? I cannot think of it. It is all on my mind.

Rachel

Jesse's regular pizza place in Southeast is crowded. Tonight it's busy with young rockers with dyed black hair and chains that hang from their belts. They'll be gone soon, Jesse says, to drag race along the wide boulevards near the college and downtown. But right now the juke box is blasting "white people music," as Lakeisha says too loudly. "Can we go someplace else?"

I agree with Lakeisha for the same reason, but say instead: "How about if we get it to go and have a picnic in a park somewhere?"

Jesse and Brick agree and walk to the counter to ask for the pizzas to go. At the counter Brick accidentally bumps one of the young rockers.

"Hey, watch it," the kid says.

"My bad," Brick says.

"Yeah, it is."

Brick is so much larger than the rocker—really than everyone else in the room—it's hard to imagine that the rocker would dare to fight him. But it's the tone in his voice that makes me think he's eager to prove to his friends, or to his girl, or to himself that he's not going to be pushed around. Not tonight.

"Okay, chill," Brick says. It's like he's used to being a target. He's the guy that you have to challenge to prove that you're not scared.

"Yeah, cool it, man," Jesse says. There's nothing more forceful or threatening in what Jesse says. But Jesse looks the rocker in the eye, and it's like they share some secret code. It's something like: He's with me. He's okay.

"Well, just tell your 'brother' to cool it. He almost knocked my pop out of my hand."

But before any of us thinks about it longer, the pizzas are ready, we run out the door. It's summer. It's a perfect summer night.

AT LAURELHURST PARK we spread out on a blanket Jesse finds in his trunk. It's hot still even though it's after dark. The sky is full of stars.

"Gotta have something to drink for a party." Jesse's bought two six-packs of beer from the grocery store with a fake ID.

"That's what I used to say," Brick says when he sees the beer.

"Well, not you, man. We should've got a root beer for you, man. Sorry."

"It's alright."

Lakeisha takes a beer and hands one to me. "I ain't gonna tell, if you don't." She opens the beer. I do too.

It is a perfect summer night, and I am sitting closer to Jesse than I normally would or maybe he's sitting closer to me.

Jesse asks a bunch of what-if questions. What if . . . what if you could live anywhere, where would it be?

"In a big old house," Lakeisha says.

"Jamaica." Jesse's choice.

"Somewhere in Europe," I say.

"Right here. This town." That's Brick.

"This is probably where I'll end up too. Working in my dad's law office," Jesse says.

We talk about everything. So we also talk about sex. The boys talk about sex. Lakeisha and I listen.

"I got my sex education from the Sears, Roebuck catalog," Jesse says. He's two beers into the night, and I can see the red rise into his cheeks. "I was like nine years old and my older cousin—he was twelve and didn't know anything. But I didn't know that then. The things he told me. Anyway, he said I could see it for myself right there in the Sears catalog. There were girls in their bras and underwear.

"I go home that day. Sneak the catalog into the bathroom with me, find the right page, and start wonking off. Then my dad opens the door. I'm like shell-shocked. He says, 'Son?' and he can see I've got the catalog open to the bigger-sized women. He says 'Excuse me, son. Go on ahead.' He closes the door and I go right back to it. That's the whole sex-ed talk he ever gave me. Guess he was just glad I wasn't gay."

We all laugh.

"Bet your grandma had a thing or two to teach you . . ." Jesse says, grinning at me.

I smile but I am glad that Brick speaks up and takes the attention away from me.

"I didn't get much of a sex-ed talk myself," Brick says. He's smiling but something is shaking in his voice.

"Come on, man," Jesse says. "What'd you need to learn? I want tips from you. Women throw themselves at you."

Lakeisha giggles.

"I'm not into that. You have to be careful with people."

Already the mood has changed. "I'm just saying," Brick says, "I was introduced to what sex was or something that—"

I can tell there is more than the secret of his age in his eyes.

"Ah, never mind," he says. "I'm making this sound like a meeting."

"Hi, my name is Brick," Jesse says. "I'm a buzz killer." Brick smiles and gives Jesse a playful shove on the shoulder. They play fight, and Brick wrestles Jesse to the ground and pins him. It's easy. Even if it is just for pretend.

IT'S GETTING CHILLY. Clouds cover the stars, but the moon is still bright. It is a bright, nearly full moon. Jesse gets his jacket for me and another blanket from his car for Lakeisha. He doesn't drape the jacket on my back like a cape, but puts it on me like a blanket and kind of tucks me in. When he sits down, and no one is looking, he puts his hand beneath the jacket, touches my knee and gives it a squeeze.

You can hear the ducks in the rushes by the pond now. And for some reason that makes us quiet. We can't see them from where we sit, but it sounds like a whole flock has landed and is settling down for the night.

"Come on," Jesse says out of the blue. "We're going to feed the ducks the leftover crusts." We run down the hill to the pond. Brick carries the box; Jesse leads the way; and Lakeisha and I trail after them.

We can hear the ducks but not see them. We each throw out several bits of crust into the water. No birds appear.

Jesse decides if they won't come to him, he'll go to them. He takes off his shoes and rolls up his shorts and walks into the water toward where they seem to be nesting.

"You crazy," Lakeisha says and takes a seat on a bench by the pond.

Jesse's in the water to his thighs. He keeps throwing bits of crust into the water, at first like coins in a wishing well, then like Frisbees across the water's top. There's a loud squawking, and suddenly a flock of birds lifts up above the rushes. They dive down to the water where Jesse stands. He's surrounded by them, and they snap up the crusts he's already thrown. "Hey, come bring me more."

Brick turns to me and extends his hand. "I don't want to get wet," I say.

"Then I'll carry you."

He kneels so that I can jump on his back, and he strides into the water where Jesse stands. He's so tall that my feet barely skim the water when he's in up to his thighs.

"Those—those are just mallards, but those over there are swans," Brick says. "If you look real close, you can see them by the tall weeds."

"I can't see them," I say.

"Then you have to listen. You'll recognize them by sound."

Brick puts his hand to his mouth and makes a bird sound like nothing I've ever heard. Once. Twice. And then the third time, the sound isn't one he's made but one that we hear.

"Oh wow. What does that sound mean?" I ask.

"It's a contact call," he says. "I guess it means, 'Hey, I'm here. I'm with you too.'"

Just then one of the swans swims through what seems like dozens of ducks to where Brick stands. We stand in the water among the birds until we have no food left to feed them. As soon as the food is gone, the birds take flight. We watch them fly away.

The boys are soaking wet. They smell like the pond. Jesse's stripped down to his boxers and has wrapped a blanket around his legs. Brick keeps wringing water from his shorts and is standing in a small puddle now. We're all shivering so we pile into Jesse's car to get warm. Jesse and I sit in the front—Brick and Lakeisha in the back. Jesse turns on the heat and then reaches into the glove compartment and takes out a pouch.

"Do you have a light?" Jesse asks Brick.

"That's drugs," Lakeisha says.

"It's harmless," Jesse says.

"It's not legal," Lakeisha says. "You could get arrested for having that."

"Shhh . . . don't tell."

"My hair's gonna smell all like that. I'm gonna get in trouble," Lakeisha says.

"Open the window. So man you got a light?"

Brick shakes his head no. Jesse rummages through the glove compartment then the side pocket on his door. He asks me to check mine too.

"How often you do that, man?" Brick asks.

"I'm casual. Not much. It's not like those people," he says.

"It's not a big deal, Brick," I say even though I'm not so sure.

Jesse finds a matchbook and lights up. I pick up a beer. It's sweaty from the heat. "Will you open this for me?" I ask Jesse.

"I'm out," Brick says.

"I'm gonna go with you," Lakeisha says.

"Rachel?" Brick looks at me.

"I'm okay. Jesse can take me home."

Lakeisha and Brick get out of the car. It is quiet for a long time after they leave, and smoke fills the air. Jesse passes the joint to me, but I wave it away. I keep drinking my beer.

"What did you mean it's not like those people?" I ask after Brick and Lakeisha are gone.

"You know, all crazy. Turn into a bum."

"Brick's not a bum."

"I wasn't saying that."

"It sounded like maybe you thought he was a bum, or even like you weren't like the men at the center because . . . It sounded like you meant black people or . . . I don't know."

"I didn't mean it that way," Jesse says. "Don't think that," he says and takes another puff. "You're not mad are you?" The way he says it is like an apology.

I don't want to be mad.

"You're different anyway, you know? It's like you're black but not really black," he says. "Don't be mad, okay? You want some? Do you want to try?" He gestures with his hand after he takes another puff.

"No," I say, but I reach for another beer.

THE SKY IS SWIRLING. And a lovely pressure rises into my head. We're lying on the ground again, watching stars. Jesse is talking about traveling: Ecuador, Peru, Argentina, Chile.

"Brazil," he says. "You know you'd look just like everyone else there."

"Really?"

"Everyone's a mulatto there basically. Brown with green eyes, gray eyes, blue eyes. It's all the same. Exotic. Those are your people," he says. "Wouldn't you love to go? To be somewhere like that?"

"Like what? A place where all the people look like me?"

My bottle of beer is empty. Jesse hands me another. I drink it like I am thirsty.

"So let's go. We'll just go," he says.

"What do you mean?"

"I'll take the check my parents gave me to pay the tuition, we'll buy a couple of tickets, and backpack all over South America. You'd love it. You'd fit right in."

"What about college?" I ask.

"When we come back, college will still be there," Jesse says.

"It's called running away," I say.

"Or it's called wanderlust," Jesse says. "Or lust."

And then he gives me a look that should not surprise me but it does. Because even though I thought that I was liking him, it seemed impossible until this moment that he was liking me too.

He leans toward me then and raises his hand to my lips. He touches me like a child touching a stranger's face. He wants to translate what is happening between us to his fingertips, make sure he can trust what he is feeling by taking me in through his hands. Are you a kind person? Well, let me feel your lips. Are they soft? His fingers move across my cheeks and my closed eyes; he's like a blind man creating me for himself. Heat grows in me in widening circles.

"Remember," he says, "I didn't come looking for this to-day." I nod my head and then kiss him—still a little distant and safe because I have not been found.

"Run!"

It's not an easy thing to do. And I'm not sure why we're doing it. But I gather my clothes up around me and pull them on real fast.

"What are we doing?" I ask.

"The sirens. Don't you hear them?"

And now I do, but before all I could hear was my heart beating fast, and his breath in my ear as he moved on top of me.

"Sirens mean danger. They mean go."

I can't tell if he's serious or not, but I rush to put my clothes on and we spill out of the car.

"Race you. To the fountain. Go."

I do everything Jesse says. I don't even think. So I run and I run faster. I run down the hill and around the tennis court and down toward the streetlights where the big fountain stands. I'm running through the dark and not scared and not out of breath. There is wind in my hair, and I feel the wind pushing me forward, like maybe I can fly. I'm at the fountain, magically still bubbling and lit. I am the first one to tag it.

"I win."

"You win," Jesse says, breathless, coming up five strides behind me.

"What's my prize?"

"This—" He splashes the fountain water with both hands hard like the top of the water's a drum. I'm covered in water— almost as wet as Jesse is—not only my shirt but my pants, my face, and my hair. He pulls me to him. We kiss. The fountain light is a bright halo behind us. Then suddenly he bends over the fountain edge and dunks his head in. Like he's being saved. When he comes up he shakes his head like a shaggy dog, and I'm wet on top of wet. "You too," he says. "Clear your head," he says. "I can't take you home looking lit up like you do now."

The part that should know that glassy eyes and smoky hair

would be easier to disguise than soaking wet clothes, wet hair, and the smell of dirty water doesn't take charge of me. Instead the part that wants to be pleasing takes the lead; it's the part of me that wants to be part of something even if it's just Jesse's crazy scheme. I lift myself up and over the edge of the fountain nearly toppling my whole self in. Hold my breath. Dip my head in the cold fountain water and come up for air with a shout. "Yee!" He kisses me again.

The sirens have died. But now there is a loud honking. Two or three cars, honking like they are speaking to each other. Loud rock music. A scream. "Nigger!"

"Nigger!" And then "Nigger lover!" Again and again and again.

"Assholes," Jesse yells. The motor revs. A screeching stop and then the powering forward sound again. And laughter. They keep laughing.

"Don't mind them," Jesse says. But I do.

BACK IN HIS car Jesse draws a map on me with his finger. He traces a line from my thigh to my chest. Travel plans. "We really could go," he says.

I feel cloudy-headed. My bad ear is drowning, like there is water in my ear that is swelling onto a shore.

"We'll go from here," he says. (My belly button is Mexico.) "To here," he says. (Somewhere near my hip bone is the Panamanian coast.) Normally I look so light—like an ivory candle next to John Bailey, next to Anthony Miller. It's the light or Jesse's very white skin that makes me brown. Or maybe it is something else. Maybe it is just words.

He draws circles within circles on my middle. He makes me brown and browner still.

"I've never done it with a black girl before," he says.

"Travel?"

"You're funny."

"Yes," I say, "I know."

Rachel

A wind inside me rises up from my feet to my head. I can feel my face grow hot.

"Good night, good night, mocha girl. My mocha girl-friend." Jesse sings the last part. "Do you want me to walk you up the stairs?"

"No, no, no," I say and hear myself talking too loudly. "I don't want my grandmother to wake up. I don't want her to see."

"I don't want to see her again like that," he says. He laughs like he is exploding.

"Good night," he sings too loud and off-key. I cannot hear the rest as I close the car door.

The wind that was rising within me swirls within my head. It makes me dizzy and unsteady on my feet. A melting feeling seems to be pulling me to the ground. I grab the railing to hold myself up. When I'm at the top of the porch stairs, I hear Jesse sing more bad notes through the open passenger window. "Mocha girl!" He honks then. He speeds away.

"Thank you Jesus, and everybody." Grandma's sitting there as if she's on her throne for Judgment Day when I open the door. She puts her hands before her in prayer.

"Little Miss, you had us worried to death."

"Us," she says, and that's when I notice Drew standing in the kitchen doorway.

"You're gonna need this," he says. He walks toward me to hand me a coffee mug.

"Look at you—a wet mess. You're gonna catch the death of you out in the night like that," Grandma says.

"Brick called me," Drew says. "He said he was worried about you."

"No need to worry. Thanks. And good night," I say and head for my room.

"Get back here, young lady," Grandma yells.

"Good night, Grandma. Good night, Drew," I say from across the room.

"Rachel?" I turn so I can see how Drew's looking at me. I'm not a kid. He knows that now.

"It's not my place to discipline you or tell you what to do. But I don't think you're doing yourself any good hanging out like you were tonight," Drew says.

"It's not your business."

"Don't talk like that. You're gonna respect Drew. You're gonna respect this house," Grandma says.

"Rachel, you have a future ahead of you. Think about it."

"You leave the mens alone, Rachel. They don't know what to do with pretty or with special. Not at your age. They don't know what you're worth."

Their voices are on top of each other. My head is spinning. I want to go to bed. I think I might get sick.

"Don't act like trash like your mama. It's not something a black girl can afford."

I can feel the blue bottle shatter inside me. "You want me to be special and you want me to be yours," I yell. "But I can't be both. You know that better than me." *Nigger, nigger, nigger lover.* "I am Nella Fløe's daughter. That's what makes me special—me."

"Tell us. Go ahead," Grandma says with a calm that she did not have seconds ago. "Tell us what a wonderful lady your mama was."

I can see Mor's face before me. Her wet eyes. Her unhappy stare.

"Go on and tell us," Grandma says. "You think that baby or Robbie or Charles would agree?"

THAT DAY THE WET air swallowed us. No fence separated the roof from the sky because no one was supposed to walk up there. The pigeon man had broken the chain lock on the door a long time ago, and we stepped out onto the rooftop where we could see the whole neighborhood.

Mor's silent misty breath seemed to fill the space between where we stood and the air before us. The wind had blown her hair into her face. It made her look messy now and not free. She led us closer and closer to the edge.

"Can we go now?" Robbie said. His face was as wet as a well-licked plate as it rained down on us.

But when Mor pushed Robbie off the roof, he didn't make a sound—he just looked at me and reached out his hand. I didn't see him fall—it was as if he surrendered to the air.

Mor came toward me next and I screamed. She stopped and looked at me. Then it was like she saw through me. She took her hand off my shoulder and turned toward the air. She stepped off the edge with Ariel in her arms and danced into the sky. They waltzed with a cloud. And for a moment I could see Mor smile.

I JUMPED AFTER Robbie then. I thought I could hurl myself over the edge and fall faster than Robbie—land before him, grab his hand, help him not be afraid.

I danced with that cloud too. I saw above me and around, beyond the day's fog. I felt my cells expanding into space and felt larger and heavier than ever before. And then I met the ground.

Heaped on top of Robbie, next to Mor and Ariel's crushed head, I lay waiting for an ambulance too. But I lived.

"I WASN'T SUPPOSED to have a future," I say. "It doesn't matter what I do. This is my life. It's my life to throw away."

Laronne

"Not a day goes by I don't think of that woman," Doug said. His face was sun-stained and wrinkled. His red hair wasn't as orange or as wooly as Laronne had remembered it; it had streaks of gray at his temples and through his trimmed goatee. He was wearing a button-down shirt and khakis. His fingernails were bitten down but clean.

"Oh?" Laronne noticed he hadn't said Nella's name.

It had been six years since the accident, and Laronne was seated before Nella's old boyfriend at a diner near her job. He drank coffee, added more sugar. He stirred.

Doug had reached her at work last week. He was working on his fourth step. He wanted to make amends. Did she know where to find Nella's grave?

"I don't know where she's buried," Laronne said. "I wanted to hear what you had to say."

Doug rubbed his eyes. He stirred the coffee some more, added more and more cream until it was light brown. Then he started to cry.

"You know, I'm changed. Been sober for close to four years now. Taking it one day at a time. I hurt a lot of people with my using. No one more than Nella. Nella was a beautiful woman. It took a long time to hit bottom after Nella was gone. I couldn't handle it. Nella saw what was good in me. I saw it in her too. I should have been better. I wasn't."

"You're a piece of shit, you know." Laronne never used that kind of language. "I should have told her that. Before."

Laronne pulled out a copy of the newspaper article about the accident and set it down in front of him.

Doug read the headline. She could see his lips move as he read. Two minutes later, she could see from the movement of his lips that he hadn't finished reading yet, but she grabbed the paper away from him anyway. "Police say they are continuing their investigation to rule out foul play. Witnesses indicate possible suspects . . ." She read the sentences as if each word had an exclamation point behind it. "So . . . ?" she asked. "They never found you. Why'd you run?"

"You think I did something? What? Are you crazy?" Doug said. "Oh my God. No. No. I wasn't there. I had already left—before."

"What are you saying?" she asked. "You came looking for her that day. At work."

"Yeah, but that was it. I didn't go back to the apartment

until the next day. After. I wasn't one for long-term," he said. "Nella knew that. We both pretended it could work. We were friends first. My first time in the program. I felt good. She'd been sober for a year and ten days. But she didn't know what happy was when I met her. It was like she was trying to make up for something. She needed fun in her life; she needed to have some fun. We had good fun. I loved her is what I'm saying, and the kind of love I had for her made her want new things. After I convinced her to move with the kids to Chicago, you know, my old friends were here. I'd go. For a night, then a night or two. I'm not proud of how I acted. I'm an alcoholic and an addict. I couldn't stay clean. And the baby. It'd cry. When I said 'get the paternity test,' I was high. It wasn't my kid. She didn't have my kid. We got into it. We . . ."

Laronne looked at him puzzled.

"It wasn't mine. I don't want you to think any less of Nella. We got together before she left him. But the baby, Ariel, wasn't mine."

It was something Laronne had guessed but never asked. It didn't matter to her.

"You know they darken up. Over time," he said.

Laronne felt her stomach tighten.

"You won't even know it," he continued. "The baby can look white when it's born and then, then—then they just get black. Black hair. Black nose. Summer makes them darker."

"Afraid you were gonna have three little *jigaboos* on your hands?" Laronne said.

"That thing—word—I said, to the kids. You say the things you've heard growing up. And I was high. It's not an excuse but it's true," Doug said. He had stopped crying. "I never took the test. I didn't think about it. A few days later, I'd been out all day with my buddy. She tells me—she says: she's his. The whole time she knew it—he'd already taken the test. And it set me off. I was going crazy. And those kids with that TV always so loud. Look, I had never hit a woman. But she kept yelling, screaming. Stay away from my babies. Get out. She wouldn't stop. I didn't mean to hurt her. I didn't think I hit her so hard until I saw she lost a tooth. I just wanted her to stop screaming. I don't mean to make excuses. What I did wasn't right. And then, you know, I left." He started to cry again. His face filled with red.

"I'll never get my chance. To make it right."

Laronne stared off into space.

Doug slid the article back to his side of the table to finish reading. He looked up, his lips still moving: "Rachel survived?"

"You don't have a right," Laronne said, "to say her name."

Nella

Day 770. Today Doug came home. I do not know why I told him — he never likes to hear Roger's name. But he is not Ariel's father. He was so mad. The children were watching TV. The TV was too loud. He was right, but he should not tell them that way. He did not have to yell. He hit the TV with his hand. Rachel did not move. The baby started crying. He pulled the TV cord out. I didn't know what to do. I was standing there. He hit Rachel on the legs with the cord. He said — he screamed at my kids — he said it: You damn little n ——.

That word.

The way Rachel looked at me. Big tears on her face. And no sound. She was a step away — maybe the step is there forever. She knows the word. She is black. I know she is not a word. If she is just a word then she doesn't have me.

I could not stop screaming. Could not stop screaming. It did not feel like anything to me when he hit me. Even when I felt my tooth being loose. I told him to get out! I screamed at him he better not ever come near my children, my family again.

My mouth stopped bleeding. Rachel cleaned the glass I threw at the door. Roger was right. That's all there is for them — only what people see. Oh God I am doing it again. I cannot do it again. I promised. Charles, I'm so sorry. I cannot be sorry again.

Rachel

I turn down the lights in the bathroom. My head is throbbing. I run the shower water and step in before it's warm. I smell like pond water. I hope Grandma can't hear me and the retching that gets rid of the spinning. Then there's sweat. I'm sweating—and I am dizzy. Sour acid's on my tongue and lips. Not the water or the toothpaste I eat rinses the taste away. I keep retching until my throat and mouth are dry. I spit. I spit again. And I grab the bar of soap and scrub my skin.

I scrub off the smell, the color, the words.

I scrub between my legs until I am raw. I scrub between my legs like I am erasing what's down there—what it makes me, what it might make.

"You, okay?" Grandma asks through the door. I keep my mouth closed. The nausea is filling me up again.

"Rachel?"

"Yes, ma'am. I'm okay, ma'am."

Grandma's feet shuffle along the wooden floor. She's at the front door, and then Drew is gone. I hear her bedroom door open and close.

I scrub. I scrub.

The water runs cold. I sit on the floor wrapped in a towel.

It's hours later when I wake up on the cold bathroom floor from a nightmare that is a memory.

The broken lock on the door.

Small steps toward the sky.

The wet air.

Robbie's face.

My mother's hands.

It's morning. I call this Day 1.

Nella

Day____. Too tired to turn the page. I cannot do it again. They're mine. If people can't see it—how can I keep them safe? In my mind is Charles all the time. All over again. He was so small. He hides in any of the places so good. He hides and we never found him. I should have took him that night—with me—he would still be alive. If I had taken Charles, he would be with me now. I will take the kids with me this time. They will go where I go.

Brick

"It's next Saturday," Brick said when Rachel opened her front door.

Brick had called every day of the last week, but she wouldn't come to the phone. She didn't come to work at the center all week. Her grandmother said she'd barely left her room because she was sick.

"Next Saturday?"

Even though the sun was before her, it looked like she was illuminated from behind. Her white dress blazed around her. And in her eyes, there was a hot blue spark.

"The amusement park?"

Brick took everything so literally. She'd forgotten. She hadn't meant it so literally.

"Oh, yeah," she said. "Where's Jesse?"

"It's just me."

She surveyed him like he was a letter delivered without a stamp. "Oh."

"Do you still want to go? You look like you're still sick."

"I'm better," she said, tugging at her ear. "Yeah, let's go."

His heart lifted. "Should I wait for you here?"

"I just need a minute."

Rachel

What I know is I am ready to go. It doesn't take long to find the blue Seagram's bag where Grandma put the two-thousand-something dollars she got for her coin collection. It's in a box in the third drawer of her dresser along with stacks of letters wrapped with ribbon. Grandma asked the coin dealer for the money in twenty-dollar bills, because that's the money she recognizes easy without her magnifying glass.

I count out fifteen hundred dollars and stick it in my jacket pocket. It's a lot of twenties and makes a fat wad.

I have already packed. I am gone.

I put the Seagram's bag back in the drawer. The letters look like they have been read over and over. Thinking they may be from Grandma's secret lover makes me almost laugh out loud.

Imagine: Grandma with a secret lizard and her naked picture shows.

I wonder who Grandma's lizard could be. I look through the envelopes, all addressed to Grandma, and see on one letter after another my father's name in the corner. I open the top one, the one that is most worn. I read:

Mama,

If you notice me there—graveside—don't let Rachel know. It's not fair to her. Let me stay gone. I can only tell her stories that she may not be ready to hear.

Thank you for helping my girl to grow up strong. The last school photo you sent, she looks sad. I hope she's not as sad as those eyes say.

Does Rachel still love to read? Will you give her this book. Nella gave it to me the year Rachel was born.

I wish I could be there to help you through. To help Rachel through. You know I would of if I could. But I am best being away.

Roger

I look at all the other letters in the drawer and don't care what they say. I put Grandma's letter back and retie the ribbon. Then I take the wad of cash out of my pocket and put it back in the bag.

"Let's go," I say as I grab Brick's arm and lock the door to Grandma's house behind me.

Brick

They arrived at Oaks Park at a quarter past twelve. It was crowded on one of the nicest Saturdays of August. Lots of sun, a cool breeze, a cloudless sky. Brick had enough for two unlimited ride bracelets, twenty-five game tickets, a hot dog or cotton candy, and two small drinks. The whole day would be his treat. He wanted to do the day proper: open doors for Rachel, give her his arm, ask her if she needed anything. Gentlemanlike.

AT THE GAME arcade Rachel took every risk. Instead of trading in game tickets she'd won, she tried for better. She tried for better every time. She wanted more—not reward but risk.

"You're on a streak of bad luck," Brick said when they were down to the last three tickets.

"I don't think so. I can feel it. My number's about to come in," she said, even though she wasn't playing a numbers game but darts. She'd missed the board completely twice. Her other throws hadn't come anywhere close to the middle rings.

The man next to her had been doing reasonably well. She turned to him and said, "Here, take these. Win something."

"Thanks," he said.

He hit the bull's-eye with the first dart Rachel's tickets provided. He hit a second and a third. Each time he made a bull's-eye he looked over to Rachel and she smiled. By the fifth, a crowd was gathering.

Rachel was the man's loudest fan. No one was as loud as she was.

He made nine. One more bull's-eye and he would win the big prize, the outsized blue bear pinned on the side wall. Bull's-eye. The crowd cheered.

"Here you go," he said, handing Rachel the bear. "For you."

"No, thank you," she said. "It's yours. You won. Congratulations." Brick and Rachel walked away.

But the man followed them. "No, it's yours," he insisted.

"I don't want it."

"Take it. Take it." He threw the stuffed animal at Rachel. His movement was so sudden and the toy so large, it nearly knocked her down. Brick grabbed the man's arm and twisted it behind his back. "Get lost."

"Your girl, she's a cocktease," the man yelled as he walked away. "You can't let her play with a man like that."

Rachel's cheeks were flushed.

"Are you okay?" Brick asked.

"It was nothing," she said. "He—he can't hurt me." And then, "Come on. I want to ride that."

"You look like you're getting sick," he said and placed the back of his hand against her forehead. "You're burning up."

All day she'd been excited like this, wildly impatient, like she'd been trapped in a husk she couldn't cast off.

"I'm fine," she said and took his hand, running toward the Haunted Kingdom ride. He knew he shouldn't go with what she said. But he did. He followed her because he would follow her anywhere now. He wanted to make her safe. "Come on, come on," she said. "It's our first grown-up ride."

As they waited in line, Brick said in a blurt, "I'm sorry. If I caused trouble for you. And for Jesse."

There was abandon in her eyes. She didn't respond.

"I just wanted to be sure you were okay. That night. It was important to me."

Something changed in her face, in her eyes—the blue spark had burned low. "I'm leaving today," she said. "I'm leaving Grandma's. Don't tell. Please."

He should have recognized it. He wanted to ask so many questions: Where are you going? When will you come back? The normal questions. He wanted to know how he could make her stay. "Let me help," he said.

"Just don't say anything."

"I won't tell," he said. "I'm good at not telling. Usually."

As the cart lurched forward through the cavernous haunted

house, mechanical mummies with glowing green eyes lunged before them. The children in the carts ahead screamed at each turn. At least one behind them had begun to cry. Nothing startled Rachel. She wasn't scared.

THERE WAS NO line at the Ferris wheel, and Brick held out his hand to help Rachel step up onto the carriage. When she still struggled, he lifted her like she was a child.

He climbed in after her. His legs leaned toward her side.

"Excuse me," he said, "they don't make these in my size." He wanted to be a gentleman. He wanted to make her smile.

The operator pushed the safety bar onto their laps. It made a click sound, and he sent them into the air slowly.

"I feel dizzy," she said.

It was the first time she'd admitted to feeling bad all day. Her face was red, and she kept wiping a thin film of sweat from her forehead with her hand.

"Hold my hand if you want," Brick said and extended his hand. She took it without looking at him.

"Does this part spin too?" Rachel asked.

"I don't think so, but I can make it rock." Brick moved back and forth in his seat making the carriage swing.

"No, please stop," she said, and he did. Her hand was still in his.

The last passengers climbed aboard. There was the click of their safety bars. Brick and Rachel were seated two carriages above the ground.

The Ferris wheel made a sound kicking into a higher gear. It began to spin.

The wheel spun so fast Rachel slid back and forth in the seat that was too small for Brick but too large for her. Her back, then her stomach pressed up against the seat and then the bar. She let go of Brick's hand. She pushed at the bar. She tugged at her ear. "I think I should get out now." She tried to stand.

"Relax. No worries. The ride's almost over."

"No, there's too much. Too much pressure." She jerked the bar to unlatch it. She covered her ear. "My ear. It hurts. It hurts."

"Calm down, okay?" Brick said.

He tried to steady her busy hands by taking them in his own. He put his arm around her. His hand was firm on her shoulder.

"I have to stand up; I have to get up." She grabbed her left ear and cradled it. She kept pushing at the safety bar.

"Okay, okay." Brick stopped fighting her. Instead he pushed as hard as she did. Harder. The bar clicked and there was enough space for her to stand. She stood with her knees slightly bent and held onto the side of the carriage. "Thank you," she said.

The operator waved at Rachel to sit down.

The wheel began to slow to a stop, Rachel was still standing and then suddenly stumbled. She would not have fallen far—their carriage was the next one to be unloaded—but Brick caught her. And it didn't matter how far the fall could have been. It mattered only that it didn't happen. Not this time.

In his arms, Rachel looked at Brick with a sadness that could not be measured.

"I know you," he said. "You survived."

Rachel

The pigeon man waves when we open the door. He shows us where he's making the new roost. Robbie's going to help. He says "p-p-p-please."

It's windy up on the roof. Robbie asks if we can go back inside. He knows we can't go yet.

Mor rocks Ariel in her arms, and Robbie and I sit real close. Mor's hair is messy, blown into her face, and tangled too. When she speaks, you can see the space for the tooth she lost in the fight with Doug. This is the third day this week Mor's brought us up here. But today she tells us stories that we haven't heard before.

Mor says there are things she can't protect us from. And she makes us all stand, and we walk closer to the edge.

She says:

"There are the regular dangers like fire."

She says:

"There are others I can't know."

We walk closer to the edge. Closer than we've ever been.

She says:

"You are my beautiful babies."

She says:

"You are the most important things in the world."

She says:

"I want to always be the best mother I can be."

She says:

"We will always be a family this way."

And I believe her.

We take small steps toward the edge. Closer. Closer.

The way people look at us. The things that people say.

She will protect us from these things too. We are closer still.

We fall.

Robbie, Mor, Ariel. Then me.

As a family, we fall.

Rachel

My hands shook as I told Brick the story. I can't imagine a time I won't cry.

"I saw your brother," Brick said, "fall."

He wiped my wet face with his hand.

"And your brother, Charles . . ." he said.

"My brother's name was Robbie," I said. "He was the one you saw."

"Your brother Charles," Brick said. "He's the one you didn't know."

Brick told me the story of Charles and of the fire in which he died. All this time I never knew that Mor and Pop had a family before me. It made a kind of sense to me then. And maybe it was also relief. Not fire or secrets or silence could keep a family from being remembered. As long as there was someone left to tell.

"What your mother did," Brick said without finishing the phrase. "Do you . . ."

"Love her?" I said. "Yeah. And I know she loved me."

My mother was my mother and she still is. *Pas på,* she'd say. *Pas på.* And I did. There was just that one time. That one day she couldn't protect me—not from the hurt and not from the words. It was just one day, but I think for Mor it seemed like Day 1.

Rachel

The park's almost empty on a cool fall afternoon. We've gone to sit by the lake at Laurelhurst Park on Brick's last day in town. Tomorrow he's going home to Chicago.

"Take this. It's a nickel from the year my dad was born," I say, handing it to him.

"It's worth a lot of money, isn't it?" he asks. "I can't." He reaches over to give it back.

"I don't need it for remembering him," I say. "You take it. A going-away present. It's worth five hundred dollars. Sell it and keep the money. I have what I need."

"Thanks," he says very softly.

We sit for a long time. Just sit there quietly. Brick flips the nickel in the air absentmindedly again and again.

A flock of birds—both ducks and swans—circles near the

water's edge to eat the bread crumbs and cakes an old woman throws nearby.

"I hope you find your mom," I say.

I'm not sure that Brick has heard me, because he takes a long time to respond.

"Me too," he says finally.

"Don't worry. You will," I say. "You found me."

Brick puts his arm around me. When he looks at me, it feels like no one has really seen me since the accident. In his eyes, I'm not the new girl. I'm not the color of my skin. I'm a story. One with a past and a future unwritten.

Brick flips the coin in the air again and again.

"You know what these are good for?" he says holding the nickel in his hand.

"What?"

"Wishes," he says. He stands then and throws the nickel into the lake.

When the coin lands in the water, it startles the feeding birds. Some squawk and swim away. Others take flight, including one awkward-looking swan that runs across the water.

"Look," I say.

The swan takes one step. Three steps, four. It dips its head and then its wings catch the wind. It's hard to tell: Is it still running or is it flying now? It's on top of the water and in the air—like it's in two worlds at once. The swan flaps its wings again and again, three times, four, and then it's aloft. We watch it fly. Away.

"Hey," Brick says finally. "What did you wish?"

"I can't tell you," I say. But I think, If only Robbie had been a bird. If only we had been a family that could fly.

ACKNOWLEDGMENTS

Thank you to Barbara Kingsolver, my hero. Thank you to Neltje, and the Jentel Artist Residency Program, where I found my voice, and thank you Mary Jane Edwards and Lynn Reeves too. I am grateful to have spent time at the New York Mills Regional Cultural Center, Hedgebrook, the Djerassi Resident Artists Program, the Ragdale Foundation, and the Ucross Foundation while working on this novel. For continued encouragement of my work I thank the New York Foundation for the Arts, Elizabeth George and the Elizabeth George Foundation, the Associated Writing Programs, the Bronx Writers' Center, the American-Scandinavian Foundation, the Lois Roth Endowment, Lorian Hemingway, Leigh Haber, the folks at Bread Loaf, Thomas Kennedy, Rowan Wilson, Helen Elaine Lee, Maurya Simon, George Hutchinson, Martyn Bone, Dorothy Allison, Maxine Clair, Whitney Otto, and Michael Pettit for his belief in what I thought was unbelievable. Thank you to my agent, Wendy Weil, for championing my work, and to my editor, Kathy Pories, for helping me find the story's shape, and to my copyeditor, Bob Jones, who helped me hone the details. Thank you to great teachers Beverly Belanger, Jeannette Swenson, Michele Stemler, Karla Hoffman, Jeff Ditzler, Carolyn Gratton, Sam Freedman, Vicki Schultz, Alan Isaacs, John Rickford, Bill Hilliard, Alex Knowles, Hettie Jones, and Joan Silber. For vision and inspiration, thank you Honorée Fannone Jeffers. Thank you to my friends for your support and encouragement over the years: Rayme Cornell, Fanshen Cox, Laurie Katz Braun, Marla Mervis, Victoria Platt Tilford, Michael Siebecker, Reg E. Cathey, Alicia Lowry, Adrienne Flagg, Brooke Campbell, Marty Hughley, Douglas Light, Murad Kalam, Jeffery R. Allen, Nova Ren Suma, and big big thanks to trusted readers Kylie Sachs, Mary Thamann, Ryan Canty, Sandy Ray, and Beena Ahmad. Thank you to Rosemary, Loretta, Michael, and Mark, and always always always Darryl E. Wash—this is for us.

050601849